HUMANS

Volume 1: The Mark

Alexandra L. Yates

ISBN: 978-1-6847-0158-2 (sc)
ISBN: 978-1-6847-0159-9 (e)

Library of Congress Control Number: 2019904253

Lulu Publishing Services rev. date: 06/07/2019

To my mother,
for giving me the confidence that with patience
and effort, everything is achievable.

KANTAS CITY

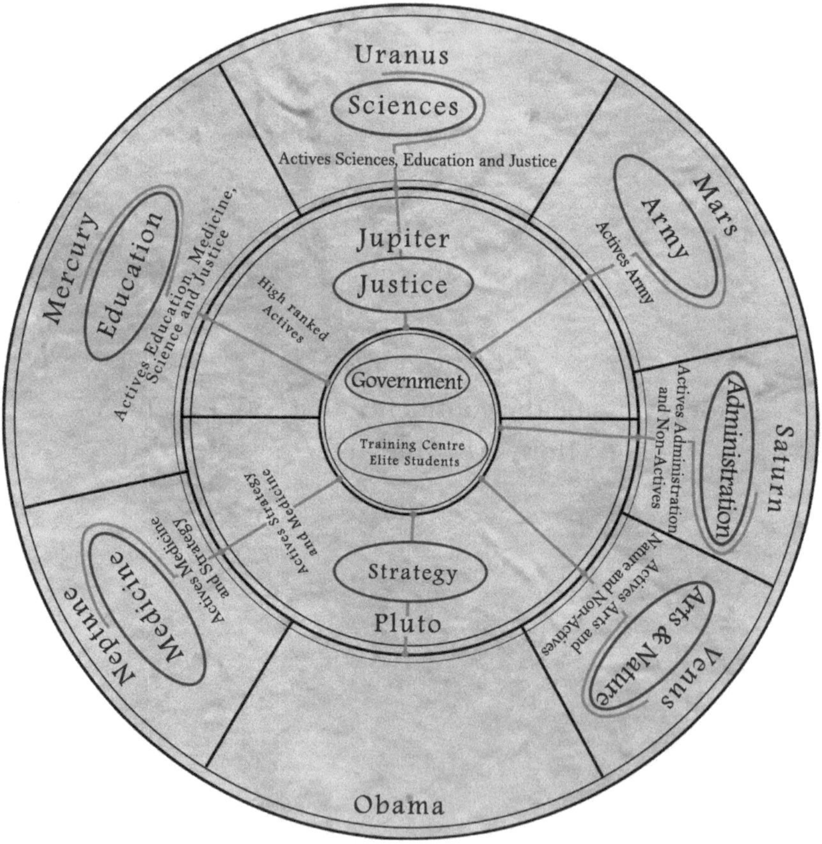

Uranus : District names

Sciences: Centers

: Train

PART 1

KANTAS CITY - YEAR 2125

CHAPTER 1

CATHY

CATHY WALKS INTO A dark room.

She inhales the lingering smell of something burning. Thick smoke engulfs her and she advances slowly, all her senses on high alert. Cathy wears an infrared mask that allows her to detect body heat and, therefore, potential enemies. However, she is surprised by a machine gun that flashes at her from her right. She throws herself to the side, while simultaneously blasting the target with her Sig 72. Before she has time to get her bearings, three men in gray combat gear attack her.

They must have used a new coating on their clothes to hide their body heat, she thinks. She is surprised for a few seconds but quickly refocuses on her goal to knock them out.

Cathy is quite tall and has strong muscles, but her opponents must still be twenty centimeters taller than her and have at least as many more pounds of muscle. In a few nanoseconds, her brain detects the weakness in each of their positions and with two uppercuts, a few cross jabs, and several sweeps, the three men are on the ground.

"Stop! Turn the lights back on."

Cathy notes the irritation in Doctor M's order. Even though the supervisors are named with letters and numbers, Cathy likes Doctor M. She has the feeling that he understands her perfectly, although he does not let her see it. It would be too dangerous for her—and also for him.

"Cathy, you were too easy on them! Look! They're already getting up."

Indeed, the three titans begin to rise to their knees. One of them immediately falls back, unconscious.

"You're exaggerating, Doctor M. They will still spend a few weeks in the hospital. I was just surprised by their new combat gear. Great technology, by the way. Congratulations!"

Doctor M looks doubtful. He knows full well that Cathy simply hates crushing these poor soldiers.

"Remember, Cathy, it's a great honor for them to come and confront one of you."

Cathy has a hard time convincing herself of that. She takes off her helmet, ties her long, blonde, wavy hair into a tight ponytail and looks at him suspiciously with her large green eyes.

"Cathy, don't even start," he says.

Dr. M glances at the cameras as if to remind her that this is neither the time nor the place to debate the issue. On the other side of the cameras there are studios where about twenty programmers and engineers, or "controllers," are analyzing her breathing, her tiniest movements, what she says, and what she sees. It is certainly not the place for Cathy to launch into a philosophical discussion about the merits of the increasing number of wounded soldiers per week just to satisfy the training of one of the members of the Elite Unit. Yet she feels that Dr. M shares some of her doubts. She definitely likes him very much.

"Come on! Join the others. They're in the Kitchen. If you don't hurry, there won't be much left for you."

Cathy turns around and starts running because, above all, she's very hungry!

She finds the others in their Kitchen, a large white room with no furniture apart from a rectangular table and eight chairs. Only their eight framed portraits—very formal and in combat uniform—decorate the place.

Leah, Stephanie, Tabitha, James, Chris, Max, and Jesse are all already seated.

A plain dish sits in the center of the table. The strong, rancid odor chokes her. And the color! Orange, brown? She doesn't care for it at all. She throws herself on the chair next to her friend Leah and fills her plate with several ladlesful.

"So, Cathy! Are you raking up your training hours? You get your ass kicked, I hope? Or did your darling Doctor M give you special treatment?" teases Jesse, a tall man with brown hair and chiseled features.

Normally, she would have tried to punch him in the face, but today her hunger is stronger. Jesse often has the gift of irritating her as soon as he opens his mouth, yet it is the taste of the food that makes her pull a face.

"Ugh. What the hell is this? It's getting more and more horrible," she says.

"Don't forget, Cathy—it's our unit that gets the most rations, the best food. And if this is the best food, I hate to think what the lower classes are getting," Leah replies in her soothing voice, putting a comforting hand on Cathy's arm. This remark calms her instantly.

Of course, Leah is right, she thinks. *There's nothing to complain about; at least we have enough to eat.* Cathy looks at one of the cameras and pretends to savor her food with exaggerated pleasure. This immediately makes Max laugh, while Stephanie looks at her sternly.

Chris, who was eagerly awaiting Cathy's arrival, like all the others, goes into telepathic mode. They are all eighteen years old and had instinctively learned to mentally converse with each other like that, right from their first meeting—ten years ago now. As everywhere else in their Training Center, their conversations are followed and scrutinized by their controllers.

"Cathy, listen," says Chris. *"Tabitha has some very important information to share with us."*

Tabitha, a stunningly beautiful young woman, the daughter of one of the leaders, always has her antennas in the air. She is, in fact, the group's informant.

"The reason why the food is so gross is that there's nothing left to eat. I heard my mother say last night that the population threshold of 100,000

in Kantas City is no longer sustainable. They're talking about bringing it down to 80,000."

In front of the cameras, everyone tries to act as if nothing is happening, but it is obvious that they are all appalled by this news.

"How many people in your slum, Cathy?" Jesse asks.

Normally one could have detected cynicism in his question, but the subject is too delicate to introduce humor—even from Jesse.

"Yesterday, there were 8,672 inhabitants in Obama. Eliminating them or throwing them out will not solve the problem," intervenes Stephanie, with her uncompromising intellectual cold-heartedness.

"We'll talk about it tonight," Chris says, cutting the conversation short. *"Max found us another underground rave. We'll discuss it quietly there."*

As she takes her last bite, Cathy looks at her gang, her family, the Eight, and suddenly finds herself taken back to ten years ago.

She was the last one to arrive in that cold white room. Her mother held her hand and kept telling her, "It's going to be okay. It's going to be okay." Yet her mother's tears and body language were telling a very different story.

"Where am I going, Mom? Why do I have to take my stuff? Why are they only taking my stuff and not yours?"

Her mother repeated, "It's going to be okay. It's going to be okay," even though Cathy had heard her screaming when the two Government men arrived at their home, accompanied by several others who were wearing riot gear and carrying batons. Some nights she was awoken by this scream, and then saw herself sitting on the well-worn red couch, surrounded by the soldiers who held her at gunpoint. They gave her mother a few minutes to pack a bag and they followed them down the stairs of their building and onto their Government shuttle. Cathy had held on firmly to her mother's hand while she kept repeating, "It's going to be okay. It's going to be okay."

Then Cathy had to let go of the warmth and softness of the hand to face the coldness of the completely white room and the seven pairs of eyes that looked at her with curiosity. A little redheaded girl, with long curly hair and freckles that made her look like a fairytale leprechaun, had approached her.

"Hello, my name is Leah. Don't be afraid. We've been waiting for you."

These words—especially the kindness that emanated from them—have remained etched in her memory. Since then she has always had a special affection for Leah who brought her comfort during one of the worst moments of her life.

She would later learn that the authorities had discussed her at length and hesitated before coming for her—even if there was no doubt about her abilities and her place among the Eight, the new Elite Unit. This unit was created every twenty-five years and included a perfect mix of children with diverse and exceptional abilities. They would later lead the largest units in the Red World and then the Government itself. Cathy's parents' past, and especially who she was, had led to long discussions within the leadership team. But in the end, the Government decided that she should be there.

She had the Mark.

CHAPTER 2

LEAH

"YOU'RE COMING WITH ME after our meal, right Cathy? I want to go with one of the shuttles that are going outside, you know. It seems they've detected a new camp and human presence. I want to go and see."

Leah contemplates the ceiling as she twirls one of her red curls. This gives her round face an even more childlike appearance. She continues with a hesitant voice.

"Maybe there are kids, you know."

Cathy cuts her off.

"Of course, Babe, I haven't forgotten. I even asked James to come with us."

Leah rushes toward Cathy and throws herself onto her with a great, big hug.

James, the blond giant with shoulders wider than the two girls combined, winks at them from the other side of the table.

"Cool! Probably some Rebels to go and smash. Always up for that!"

Leah thinks especially of the children, of those helpless creatures, victims of a world that they don't understand. Even as a child, Leah never missed an opportunity to slip away from her parents or to sneak out of her Education Center, to go to the Obama district. There, she went in search of destitute children whom she would use as her patients to practice one. Her parents always found her kneeling over one of them, eyes closed, slowly running her hands over their wounds. They would discretely take her home, lecturing her, "You are special, Leah. If members of the Government know what you are doing, they will not allow you to join the new Elite Class. You've got the Mark, Leah. You've got the Mark."

But Leah couldn't understand why her parents, although being high-ranking figures in the Justice Operations Center, would not want her to help these poor, sick children. At only five years of age, she could already cure them.

The bell rings at the end of the meal and everyone rushes to the dressing room. It is a large gray room with lockers in which their various uniforms are neatly folded, together with some of their combat weapons. There is always a musty smell because the showers are directly adjacent, without any ventilation. These boys and girls have already been sharing everything for ten years and there is no room for modesty or secrets.

Cathy, Leah, and James put on their outdoor combat suits, specially designed to protect them from radiation and extreme cold. No one knows in advance their destination.

"Don't forget to take your daggers, you never know. A little close-combat session would be fun!" says James.

What could be more exciting than getting out of their Dome?

"I took my AK-47. It's going to be fun," Cathy says with a big smile.

Her assault rifle has, of course, little to do with the Kalashnikovs used during the guerrilla campaigns before the Ecological Wars, but the Eight like to use old names to call their weapons.

Leah listens distractedly. There have been several raids in recent months in search of Rebel camps. *The Government seems nervous,* she thinks, and she is worried about what happens during these raids. Whenever she can, she uses her status and privileges to go on the raids. And every time, she's grateful Cathy is with her. *Cathy is so strong: she will always know what to do.*

With a quick pace, they reach the nearest elevator taking them to the roof of their building, where a helicopter awaits them and will transport them to one of the exit points of the Dome surrounding Kantas City.

In the helicopter, Leah looks at the city. Everything appears so orderly to her, so cold, so gray—especially this Dome above them. It may be transparent, but it makes her feel like she's in a prison. She shakes her head while addressing her friends.

"The North Exit. They could have called it the Gate of Freedom, or the Gate of Liberation. What a lack of imagination!"

James and Cathy burst out laughing. If there is one quality that the Founders of the Red World or the current Government do not have, it is imagination. Everything is so meticulously ordered and organized.

The helicopter lands near a transport shuttle where six members of the Special Forces are lined up in a row. The pilot is already inside, ready to take off. Leah, Cathy, and James quickly greet them and leave to settle down in the shuttle.

The aircraft glides slowly through several security airlocks that open and close as they pass. From the control room, the gate guards confirm and reconfirm the transit of the ten passengers by checking that no other human has passed. Exiting or entering Kantas City is a most delicate and controlled operation.

A few minutes have passed and the shuttle is finally leaving the Dome. Even after several excursions outside Kantas City, no one gets tired of looking at the cupola from the outside, an architectural wonder of great scale covering a city where skyscrapers, gardens, and residential districts mingle. Around the protected city there only remains an arid, icy, and burned landscape, where winds that seem to have lost their sense of direction whirl round and raise a thick, yellow dust. Cathy sometimes wonders how the people regularly expelled from the city, in the name of the Red World's sustainability, manage to survive in this hell. Her daydream is interrupted by Leah's little voice, which creeps into her mind via telepathy.

"I heard that this time they were almost certain they had spotted Rebels."

"Jesse's mother told him that the Government is getting more and more nervous," adds James. "Reports indicate increasing numbers of

survivors—foragers who have adapted to the environment. According to the reports, many of them join the Rebels."

"Their growing numbers could become a threat," says Leah. *"And there are rumors circulating that the mission of these short excursions is to eliminate any form of life within a radius of 300 kilometers around the Dome."*

"I wouldn't be surprised," replies Cathy. *"The guys who are with us are some of the best in Special Forces. I remember having observed some of them during their training sessions. Their leader who's sitting next to me is a real, bad person. Really, a very bad person."*

While continuing their telepathic conversation, their faces appear to others as inexpressive as if they were asleep. *"I don't like it,"* Leah tells them. *"All investments go into the army and yet there is nothing left to eat. Couldn't they speed up food research instead?"*

"Yes, even my parents say that—and they usually believe what they're told. We've all seen that there's something wrong," James says. *"How long has it been? Six months they've been freaking out?"*

"Okay, guys, let's focus now," Cathy tells them. *"Look in front of you: I think we've arrived!"*

They have only been gone for about twenty minutes and have just passed a rugged mountain range, and yet they have already flown over three hundred kilometers from the Dome. What they see in front of them takes their breath away. As if taken from an old photo of the 20th century and well hidden in a valley, an old railway station emerges, a hundred meters long. Dozens of rails leave each side, through four separate tunnels. The main building contains at least a hundred windows, most of which are obviously destroyed. In its center, a grand entrance of about twenty meters dominates the whole structure. That a building like this could still be standing is a mystery. Probably it survived because of its location in this deep valley, protected by the majestic peaks. Cathy, James, and Leah don't hide their pleasure at being in front of an old 20th-century building like so many they have seen in the archives of Kantas City.

"If Stephanie were here, she could tell us what this building is. Its size and location are not common," James continues telepathically.

At this point, the shuttle lands gently and the one whom Cathy identifies as the leader of the group signals them all to turn on their radios.

"I'm Captain 212, commander of this expedition. You and you," he says, pointing to two of his subordinates. "You will stay close to the shuttle to guard it and protect the pilot. The others, you're coming with me."

"And," he adds, after a pause and a strange face, as if it pains him to continue, "The Three Elites, you follow us. But be careful, no nonsense, kids. You're here as mere observers. I'm in charge here. And you should know it pisses me off that you're here!"

"Aye, aye, Captain!" Cathy answers quickly.

Leah and James refrain from laughing. If there's anyone Cathy would never follow orders from, it's a Special Forces Captain.

The military men advance with great caution towards the building. It's pretty cold and there's no sign of harmful vapors around them. They do not need their activity sensor to recognize that there is indeed human activity in the building. Scrap metal hangs here and there, fabrics hanging from some windows, probably a vain attempt to insulate it from a cold that must be icy every night, given the altitude and isolation of the valley.

Even with their suits on, Leah, James, and Cathy shivered when they left the shuttle. Leah goes into telepathy mode as she enters the building. *"If there are children here, imagine the conditions they live in."*

Around them lay piles of debris and a few haphazard tents. No sign of human presence. They must have gone into hiding as soon as they heard the shuttle approaching.

"Actually, it's not that bad," Cathy says. *"It's a good thing some buildings like this have survived. At least they are protected from acid rain and the temperature is really better here."*

James interrupts them. *"Girls, I don't trust the idiots in front. Get ready, okay?"*

Just then, a ragged four-year-old boy runs out of a tent. A panic-stricken woman immediately runs out in a desperate attempt to catch him. The Captain calmly raises his arm, tracks the woman with his gun, and shoots her. Leah has already set off, running as fast as she can, hides the child behind her back, and holds the captain at gunpoint. Cathy and James have already positioned themselves around the four soldiers, their weapons clearly visible and ready to use. Finally, James has activated a signal jammer—a gadget prepared by Chris to make sure that what happens now will neither be heard by the military men outside nor recorded.

"What are you kids doing?" The Captain is unnerved. "You think you're on a humanitarian mission or something? You don't understand anything. We're going to have to kill them all. Those are the orders!"

"And you think we're going to follow your orders, you dumb-ass?" Cathy answers.

Cathy, Leah, and James look at each other for a few seconds. Long enough to share their pain but also their determination. They are not happy about the actions that will follow, but for them, at least, they are the right ones.

Simultaneously—as if one person—James and Cathy shoot the four soldiers.

Cathy, James, and Leah have felt all the eyes hiding around them and wonder how the inhabitants will react to the scene they have just witnessed.

A few seconds pass. Leah still holds the child in her arms. He has obviously been calmed by her warmth and gentleness. Cathy and James are waiting for something to happen. What happens next is quite unexpected.

"Cathy, Leah, look at the sky!" James tells them. "Leah, do you know how to control the sky or what?" he laughs.

Sun rays enter through the windows. The main hall, which a few seconds earlier was gray, cold, and impregnated with a musty smell, is now bright. Even the ambient odor is changing; a scent of burning spreads around them. The remains of grandiose frescos are now visible on the ceilings, where angels seem to float on clouds white as snow. Leah, Cathy, and James stand dazzled, watching the show made even more surreal as a hundred of men, women, and children slowly leave their various doors and shelters. They all wear animal furs. Their movement is agile, a sign of great physical dexterity, probably made necessary by their mode of survival.

"Cathy? What do you feel?" Leah asks telepathically.

"I feel no animosity, but above all, I see in them a beautiful morality. They're foragers," Cathy says.

"It's fascinating. Where did they come from? How do they survive?" asks James.

A very old man comes closer to them and falls to his knees in a clear sign of respect. The rest of the assembly follow his action.

"Damn! Do they think we are gods or what?" James asks his two friends.

Cathy steps up to the old man, stows her gun and with a loud, confident voice speaks to them.

"I'm Cathy. My friends here are Leah and James. The Red World has detected your presence and we have come with some men from the Red Army. To protect you, we had no choice but to eliminate them. But you should know that our intentions are peaceful."

Cathy stops, waiting for a sign that she doesn't yet see.

"We brought you some medicine and vitamins from Kantas City."

The old man, probably their leader, does not answer but nods, allowing Cathy to continue. Cathy, Leah, and James put their weapons away and take dozens of small bags out of different pockets and gently drop them on the floor.

"We'll take the bodies, and we'll find a way to explain this accident."

Then Cathy adds:

"But we would like to come back one day with our friends, to take the time to talk with you."

The old man still does not say a word. Instead, he makes a sign to a young girl, who runs off. A few seconds later, she returns with two small bundles of cloth and gives them to the old man.

"That's not possible! They must also master telepathy. Unbelievable!" James says to the girls.

The Eight are, to their knowledge, the only ones who can master this art in the Red World. Even previous generations of Elite students couldn't communicate like that.

The old man opens the first bundle of cloth and presents them with what appears to be fruits.

"Grapes?" Cathy asks.

The old man nods.

Cathy takes the treasure with great care, divides the few grapes from the bunch perfectly into three, and gives some to Leah and James. Leah's hands are almost shaking. Tasting grapes, fruit in general, is so rare. *Where did they grow them*? ask the three to themselves. When they put the first grape in their mouths and crunch the skin around it, the acidic pulp spreads down their throats and they cannot help closing their eyes for a few moments. They repeat the same ritual four times and then the old man smiles at them, showing his toothless grin. James, Leah and Cathy smile back at him.

"Thank you for your wonderful gift," Cathy says to him with great respect.

He then approaches Leah and presents her with the second bundle of fabric. Leah has now released the boy, but he still clings to her leg. She opens the fabric and discovers a statuette. It is no more than five inches high and depicts a naked woman. She must be very important to the community because when the whole assembly sees her, they get down on their knees. Leah, quite naturally, kisses the effigy and delicately puts it in one of the inside pockets of her suit.

"Leah, you're going to have to explain to us what you're doing. Did you really just kiss the statue? But first, girls, we have to get out of here pretty quickly and get the four bodies back," James suggests telepathically.

"Thank you, Great Chief," says Leah. "We'll take good care of it."

"We're going to have to leave now," Cathy says loud and clear. "But we'll be back with our friends very soon."

Leah tightly hugs the child who is still close to her, then pulls herself away with great sadness. James grabs two soldiers by the legs, followed by Leah and Cathy who take care of the other two.

As soon as they pull the four bodies out of the building, the sun disappears behind a gray cloud. It's as if the stage were closing behind them, the icy cold reclaiming its rights.

"Well, now we're going to have to deal with the other two," Cathy says.

"Are you sure we can trust the pilot?" asks James. "I can fly the shuttle without any problem. But frankly, if we don't take care of him, we're running a hell of a risk."

"He's safe. I'll check again but the diagnosis I made on the way was really positive. I even think he can become a key ally for the future."

"He is certainly an excellent pilot," adds James.

"You know Cathy, I, too, felt that there were no violent feelings between these humans," interrupts Leah.

"Maybe they're not exactly our kind. There was something different about them," James ponders.

"That's what I keep thinking, too," Cathy says. "We'll have to come back here, that's for sure. And very quickly, because I don't get the impression that they're the type that stays in one place. Especially not after what just happened."

As they advance towards the shuttle, pulling the corpses behind them, the two soldiers and the pilot approach. Their hesitant gait reveals how worried they are when they see the young people coming towards them, especially as they see James nonchalantly pulling the two corpses.

"Hey, guys, how ya doin'?" James asks them as he drops the two bodies.

"You can take them both," Cathy says to James. "They're garbage."

Before the two soldiers can do anything, James pulls out two guns and shoots them in the head. Leah and Cathy hold the pilot at gunpoint.

"Oh my God, kids, what the hell are you doing?" screams the pilot, totally panicked.

"Two less psychopaths. Good riddance!" exclaims James.

"It is clear that the Red World doesn't suffer from a lack psychos," says Leah in a disillusioned voice.

"So, what's your verdict, Cathy?" asks James who now has the pilot in the sights of his gun.

Cathy concentrates and probes the person in front of her. She has this extraordinary gift, unique among the Eight, to be able to read the psychological profile and evaluate the morality of a person just by looking at them. She's taking her time because James is right—she can't take any chances. Their survival, all Eight of them, is at stake.

"Oh, he's beautiful, unfailingly ethical," says Cathy with a smile. "A little stubborn and twisted on the edges but he hates the Red Army as much as we do. Moreover, it is quite exceptional that he was able to reach such a high rank without being noticed."

The pilot looks at them without understanding. "Aren't you from the new Elite class?"

Leah replies with a smile. "Oh, yes! They must have screwed up the recruitment somewhere!"

And she adds, using her calm voice which would soften even the most hard-hearted:

"What's your name, Pilot?"

The pilot is stunned.

"I'm P923."

He looks at all three of them and then exclaims out loud as if to himself: "Okay, I have nothing left to lose! I'm also known as Noah."

Except for the Elites, no one in the Red World has a designated first name, so a first name can therefore only belong to a Rebel.

"Excellent, Noah!" exclaims Cathy. "Now we're going to manage the situation. We're going to go back and land near a ravine. You and James will reset the onboard computer to erase this location while Leah and I will dump the bodies overboard and create an explosion so they're well buried. Then, we'll go innocently home and tell Jesse and Tabitha to ask their parents to cover it up."

"Yes, well, seeing us come back every time without soldiers, they're going to start to suspect something," James replies sarcastically.

All three know that they are playing with fire and that their situation is becoming more and more delicate.

"No problem," says Noah. "You can count on me. What just happened will remain a secret between us. I swear it."

Leah, James, and Cathy know it's not an empty promise. He will undoubtedly have to report on his return and go through one of Kantas City's secret torture rooms.

"Come on, let's go!" exclaims James. "We have to get home in time for our night out. I really want to see Max have some fun."

CHAPTER 3

MAX

"MAX, FOR ONCE WE have permission to go out. Do you want to go home first, or shall we go straight to Cathy's?" asks Jesse.

Max catches his breath before answering.

"I don't care about going home. How about you? Why don't we go straight there?"

"Yeah, that works for me. That way, I still have an hour to kick your ass." Then he adds telepathically, *"That will allow me to avoid meeting my father."*

The two friends look at each other conspiratorially.

"You know I'll always be the best at karate," Max tells him.

"In your dreams," Jesse replies, smiling.

After a few more exercises, they reach their locker room. "Hey Jesse, what do you think about these Rebel stories? I'm looking forward to hearing all about this afternoon's expedition," says Max.

Jesse combs his straight brown hair back and stares at Max with his gray, ice-cold eyes. Jesse is his friend and Max can understand the nuances of his eyes, which can't be said of everyone who meets him and is automatically intimidated.

"I think there is something very important going on."

Jesse continues telepathically. *"I've never seen my father like this. Frankly, Max, he's even worse than usual. He could kill anyone who comes near him."*

Max replies. *"You think it's because they're proposing to reduce the population threshold to 80,000?"*

"Are you kidding? He doesn't give a shit; he gets a sick pleasure out of expelling people from Kantas City. No, I'd have to get him to talk. But given how we're getting on, it's not a sure thing. I think there's something else going on and it's connected to the Rebels."

Max answers him, this time aloud, "It can't be much, right?"

"You're right, buddy!" Then Jesse adds mischievously, "It's time to go see the freaks in Cathy's neighborhood."

Max gives him a good pat on the back and they both leave to take the train that connects the districts of Kantas City.

There are only three stops before they reach the entrance of the Obama district, but the contrast with the rest of the city is striking. The train does not go any further. Apart from the employees of the Education or Medicine Units, no other inhabitant would want to set foot there. So, what's the point of having a train? Indeed, it is surely the most dangerous place in the city, where the poor intermingle with the excluded and those trying to hide from the Red World Police. The district had been named for a black president who was famous long before the Ecological Wars, which permanently ravaged the planet and eliminated more than 99.99 % of the population. The neighborhood has a bad reputation and few dare to venture there. But Cathy's mother lives there and the Eight often meet there. It has been their favorite playground for ten years, to the great displeasure of their instructors who have no control over them there.

Max and Jesse jump off the train and jog down a run-down street. At this pace, it only takes them about ten minutes to reach Cathy's mother's building. It is not only the appearance of the buildings that differs from those of the other districts, which are immaculate; there is also the ambient odor, due to the water treatment system, which is definitely less than optimal. They pass some groups that greet them with a nod. They come and go as they please for two reasons: one, Max and Jesse wear their Elite student uniforms, the most selective and prestigious squadron in the Red World; and two, the reputation of the Eight has been well-known for a long time throughout Obama.

The building where Cathy's mother lives is now in sight. It's a five-story block, as old as Kantas City, but obviously no longer looked after. In the windows, panes of glass are missing and have been replaced with cardboard or fabric. A feeling of sadness and misery emanates from it, as from the whole district. But the inhabitants, like the Eight, don't see it that way. Instead, Max feels excitement as he climbs the stairs as fast as possible to reach the top floor and join his friends. Cathy's mother opens the door and lets them in with indifference. She has been a ghost of her former self for some time now. The others are all there. Cathy, Leah, and James came directly from the North Exit where the shuttle dropped them off. After a simple briefing, they were able to leave as if nothing had happened. Stephanie, Tabitha, and Chris had run there a little earlier, as if on a training run.

Chris starts fiddling with his computer and then moves towards Cathy's mother, sitting as always in front of her only window, looking out and rocking herself now and then. "Mother, I'm going to leave you our transmitter boxes as usual. You'll move them from time to time, won't you?"

Cathy's mother smiles at him. Even in her madness, she loves Cathy and her friends. "I'll move the boxes, making it look like you're in the bathroom and in bed." She starts laughing like a child.

Leah approaches her and kisses her on the forehead. Chris can't help but feel a tug in his heart as he watches the scene.

Now Chris has activated the signal jammer. He invented this system a few years ago so that they could talk to each other in private, even on the grounds of their training camp. So far, their ploy has not been discovered. This is obviously an additional precaution, given that their controllers can no longer listen to them in this neighborhood. Now he can ask aloud for news of the expedition.

"So? What did you find?" he asks impatiently.

James starts:

"First, we left with six members of the Special Forces, and not the least awful but the worst kind."

Leah continues:

"We arrived in front of a building, hidden in mountains, at the bottom of a valley. It looked like the images of the international station at Canfranc, which we studied during our course on the old transportation systems. Remember, Stephanie?"

"That's fascinating! This would mean that it might be in what used to be France or Spain since the station was on the border. According to my calculations, you couldn't have traveled more than 300 kilometers," Stephanie replies, excitedly.

"Be careful, Stephanie, we're not sure. However, there are traces of ancient religious frescoes and that should really interest you, Max and Stephanie," says Leah.

"Okay, so what happened after that?" Jesse asks, obviously not interested in ancient art.

"There was evidence of inhabitants," James continues. "We were with four soldiers in the compound. When a child came out of a shelter, followed by a woman, and the Commander killed her, it was very clear to us that we were not there on a humanitarian visit."

"And what did you do?" asks Chris in a tone that clearly indicates that he knows the answer.

"We shot all four of them like the mad dogs they were," Cathy says.

At the sound of Cathy's voice, her mother turns suddenly towards her, her eyes full of sadness. Cathy shakes her head.

"They were the worst kind, Mom. I know that they, themselves, killed and tortured so many people and, unfortunately, they would have continued. We had no choice," she says, trying to justify the unjustifiable.

No one dares add anything for a few seconds. The weight of the guilt and the secrets they share is often too heavy to bear.

Finally, Leah decides to interrupt this moment of unease.

"As I was protecting the child, a hundred people came out and the old man, who was obviously the chief, gave me this," she says, taking out the small, carved object in the shape of a woman. "It seemed very valuable to them."

"Yes, they even seemed to worship Leah!" adds James.

"Who doesn't worship Leah?" says Chris teasingly.

"The most fascinating thing about all this is that..." says Cathy, with a pause for effect, "...they were all pure. No sign of violence in them."

"You're talking nonsense," Jesse says.

"Even I felt it. It was amazing," adds Leah.

"And they even gave us grapes to taste! Can you imagine, grapes! No idea where they came from," James exclaims.

Jesse looks at them suspiciously and adds:

"We're all going to have to go there for sure! How did you get home?"

"We had to start by eliminating the other two soldiers, who stayed close to the shuttle. But we spared the pilot. Cathy realized that he was a Rebel, named Noah," adds James.

"The only Rebel in the story was actually the pilot in the shuttle," jokes Max.

Tabitha, who hasn't said a word since the beginning of the conversation, interjects in a dry tone. "It also means we're going to have to ask my mom to cover this up again, right?"

"That would be nice indeed, Tab," says Leah, with her most beautiful smile.

"Yes, I'm avoiding my father right now," Jesse adds. "He's in a killing mood!"

Everybody looks at him. That Jesse's father isn't in a good mood is never a good sign. He is one of the eight leaders in charge of the Army, and he is by far the most dangerous in the Government.

Max, who doesn't want the evening to be ruined by any gloom, says in a cheerful voice to his friends:

"Come on, let's get changed! Mother, do you have our clothes, please?"

Cathy's mother gets an old bag that she has carefully hidden, and gives them their Obama clothes, as well as new clothes she has prepared for them. Once dressed, all in black, with their torn clothes and raised hoodies, they look like all the other rejects from the district. Following Max, they take the service stairs, a final precaution against their controllers.

Max and Cathy walk ahead, without saying anything, just enjoying themselves.

Max enjoys the feeling of freedom, just like every other time he takes off his uniform. They are no longer the Eight Elite. They are only a group of eighteen-year-old friends, going out to have fun. The violence James described on their excursion this afternoon left a bitter taste in his mouth that he tries to forget. Unfortunately, he knows the members of the Special Forces all too well. What an irony that his parents were Special Forces, he who hates violence more than anyone. And especially what a disappointment it was for them, when he began to be much more interested in nature and the arts, than fighting with his neighborhood friends. His neighborhood, called Mars, contains all the Army personnel, and the fights in the sandboxes are the first important tests for these children. Of course, even when he was small Max was already very strong, and had no problem defending himself, but the adults around him were not fooled, much to the shame of his parents. "Psychopaths," he says to himself angrily. Of the Eight, he and Leah are the ones who least tolerate the little value that the Government and Army personnel place on human life, and more and more he finds himself dreaming of somewhere else, of another world. What if this other world existed?

Meanwhile, tonight, he is hoping to escape, if only in his head.

When they meet other groups, mostly of young people at this time of day, they all defer to Cathy. Max knows that Cathy is strong and that she has been able to make her authority felt in this district where the Government has always had difficulty imposing its law. But he is always impressed by the respect she receives. Max can still see her clearly from years ago, covered with wounds and bruises, on her return from visits to her mother. She never complained. And he also knows that color all too well. It had so often covered his body, until the day he became strong enough to knock his father out.

On impulse, spurred by these memories, Max clasps Cathy by the neck and gives her a kiss on her head, through her hoodie. The rest of them laugh, wondering what the hell got into him.

They finally arrive in front of a building that also seems to be collapsing. Four men are sitting there. When they arrive, one of them moves towards Cathy and Max. "Hi Cathy," he says, and he hands Max a screen while staring at Cathy.

Max types the code and the four giants let them through. Behind the door, several young women with colorful hair and extravagant outfits are waiting for them. The Eight quickly remove their black tracksuits and reveal a whole new look. Tabitha and Leah are particularly glowing, while Cathy and Stephanie, as usual, have worn dark suits.

"Cathy's mother is definitely a great seamstress," Chris says.

"How does she find these colored fabrics?" asks Max.

Cathy smiles with pleasure and her green eyes take on a golden glow.

Drum sounds can be heard in the distance. Stephanie is getting closer to Cathy. "Are you sure they were pure? I can't get it out of my head."

"Yes, Stephanie. It was incredible. I felt no psychopathic, sadistic, or manipulative inclination," answers Cathy.

"Maybe your superpowers are starting to fade as you get older," Jesse laughs.

Leah intervenes. "Stop it, Jesse, you're so annoying."

Stephanie continues as if nothing had happened, lost in her thoughts.

"Either they are not of our species, with a different DNA, or they have not yet been in contact with our culture. This would mean that violence in our society is only the product of our culture and propaganda."

"Okay, okay, Stephanie. We're all going to go. This is really starting to intrigue me," Jesse says teasingly as he looks at Cathy.

Cathy sticks out her tongue, smiling. Jesse looks at her, surprised. Max taps him on the shoulder.

"That's what this evening does to us. Even Cathy is in a playful mood."

And pumping his fist in the air, he adds, "Let's go, folks!"

As they advance, the music gets louder and louder. They still have two buildings to cross and a few stairs to take, before arriving in a room that looks like an old hangar, where a hundred people are dancing. Max cannot contain his pleasure and shouts with excitement. There's everything he loves. In fact, everything that is forbidden in the Red World: music, young people gathered together and from all horizons. There is color everywhere, in clothes and on walls, and also love.

They have been going to these parties for two years now. The appointments are fixed a few days beforehand, by a system of codes that only a few insiders can decrypt. These parties are not an urban legend and Max has done everything so that his group of friends, the Eight, could be part of them. Young people come from all walks of life, although the vast majority are from the Obama district, and they can finally forget their world—The Red World—thanks to music and, for some, illegal drinks. Elite students relish above all the pleasure of freedom.

Max approaches the makeshift stage and takes the guitar that is waiting for him, resting against rusty old tanks that delineate the space. Some have "No Nukes" stickers, signs from a former environmental organization called Greenpeace. What an irony, Max thinks, knowing that the world is as it is today because of the nuclear explosions of 2025 that this organization had fought so hard to prevent.

Max starts playing some chords on a guitar and the DJ launches into electro music from the last century, his looper next to him. A young woman, whom Max has already seen several times, goes up on stage and starts beating on the tanks like drums. The DJ raises the volume gradually, as they all play together. Spirits then become one with the music and the bodies move to the rhythm of the sound that rises and falls.

Max has dark blond hair, a round face with a prominent forehead, a heart-shaped mouth, a rounded chin, some freckles on his face. His eyes are swollen with lack of sleep, which gives his hazelnut gaze even more intensity. Fingers worn by the instruments twirl elegantly on the guitar and even if he is not very tall—he is smaller than James or Jesse—it is difficult not to be hypnotized by Max's charisma and intensity. As always, the whole room has eyes only for him.

Time flies. Minutes or hours?

Some drink, all dance.

It's a long night. It's hot; they're all drunk from pleasure.

Suddenly a siren sounds.

Max hastily puts down the guitar and the seven others join him laughing and congratulating him. They will now have to leave, hide from the Army, which can't be far away, and return as soon as possible to Cathy's mother. But they are not worried. The Obama district is their playground, theirs and the other young people's around them. There's little chance the Army can catch anyone.

What a perfect night, Max thinks.

CHAPTER 4

TABITHA

THEY ONLY SLEPT A few hours, but thanks to their training they are all in great shape. The meditation exercises they practice during the day provide them with the rest they need.

Tabitha has already contacted her mother, and they decided to meet this morning. Then she'll join the others at the Training Center. She leaves her friends at the entrance of the Obama district and takes the train in a different direction. With her Elite uniform, slender figure, dark skin, long black hair, big hazel eyes, fine nose, and luscious lips, she is truly superb and striking in any crowd.

Her demeanor is full of confidence. The platforms and trains are completely crowded at this hour, and the workers and children, Actives and Non-Actives, clear her path and leave her as much space as possible. They're all looking at her with sideways glances. Tabitha doesn't even care anymore. It has always been like that. She is Ariane's daughter, she is an Elite, and she is beautiful—many reasons to attract all the attention.

Tabitha rehearses again and again in her head the conversation she's going to have with her mother. This is an impossible situation. *What is the probability that only the military personnel were killed in the accident? And above all, there was the pilot, who certainly had to undergo a tough interrogation session. Will he be strong enough not to turn his friends in?* Tabitha drills James, Leah, and Cathy. *James and Leah are too kind, too compassionate,* she thinks. *But Cathy? She should know that she should not take any risks. She, above all, is subject to even closer controls than all other Elite students.*

The train stops in front of the Mercury entrance. The scene repeats itself: all the passengers crush tighter together to clear a path for the one that many call the Princess. Tabitha walks through the crowd, without noticing anyone, concentrating on her mother. A few dozen meters from them, she rests, nonchalantly, on her little racing car—a gray, flying sphere with three-meter wings on each side, and able to transport up to five people. Having your own shuttle is the privilege of former Elite students, who have become the leaders of the Government.

If the crowd is breathless at the sight of Princess Tabitha, so too are they when looking at her mother Ariane.

Ariane is Tabitha plus a few more years: tall, the same amazing dark skin, proud features, and large hazel eyes. The only difference with Tabitha is a short haircut, a sign of maturity. Above all, she has a certain roundness in her face that gives her a very soft look. Tabitha looks at her and, as always, thinks that her mother is not what she seems to be.

"Hello, Mother," Tabitha says, quickly embracing her.

"Hello, Daughter." Ariane lets Tabitha sit next to her in the car, and says, "I'm taking you to an Education Center."

She starts her flying car with an expert hand. Ariane usually takes her daughter to one of her Organization's Centers when she needs to have a serious discussion with her.

The car launches gently into the air. Tabitha, like her mother, loves to fly. It is one of the many advantages of being an Elite, and she never tires of looking at Kantas City, with its Dome of Protection above. The Mercury district is perfectly ordered with its white houses where the Actives in the Centers of Education, Medicine, Science, and Justice live. Also in this district are the Education Centers, while the Neptune district, next door, contains the Medical Centers and is where most of the Medical and Strategy Actives live. On the other side of the district is the Uranus district, with its Science Centers and where the Actives of Science, Education, and Justice reside. The other district in the vicinity, towards the city center, is the Jupiter district which houses the Justice Centers. This is where the city's high-ranking and privileged people live.

The car lands in front of a large white building. Several guards waiting in front rush to open the door for Ariane, the Leader of the Education Centers, and her daughter. Military personnel are also there to escort them through the corridors, which, like many in Kantas City, are completely white, unless they are gradient shades of black, gray, or beige.

On either side of the corridor are classes for children under ten years of age. Tabitha takes the opportunity to put her extraordinary hearing to work and listens through the doors to the noises in the different classes. Some are repeating what their teacher tells them, other classes are very quiet, in yet others she perceives the joyful laughter of children. Ariane suddenly stops in front of a door, identical to all the others, and chooses to enter a class where a dozen little faces raise big smiling eyes towards them. Tabitha, who usually looks so cold and arrogant, can't help but soften at the sight of these innocent faces. She estimates that they must be around eight years old because she remembers well having been in one of these classes.

Everything was so easy then, she thinks. Especially being Ariane's daughter. Everyone wanted to be her friend. She was spoiled and lived in Ariane's large and beautiful house in Jupiter. She remembers meeting her friends ten years ago after they had all been taken together to their special Training Center. They were no longer as smiling because they knew they would receive an education that was more intense and demanding than anything experienced by the other children in Kantas City.

Ariane walks up to the teacher, a young woman in her thirties who looks scholarly with her round face, big glasses, and curly black hair. With a gentle gesture, Ariane takes her arm and sits next to her.

Tabitha sits discreetly among the little ones, who look at her with surprise.

"What have you children learned today?" asks Ariane.

All the children raise their hands. The teacher points to a little girl with long black hair that could be Chris' little sister.

"We learned why, before the Ecological Wars, people believed that there were racial differences and how the Red World eliminated this concept."

Tabitha jolts imperceptibly.

"Before, some people thought that people were different if they didn't have the same color of skin," continues the little girl.

Tabitha wonders if Ariane has organized this little display in advance, as usual, or if it is just pure chance that they find themselves in this class, as she knows that this subject is as sensitive for Ariane as it is for her.

"Have you studied the history of the United States, children?" asks Ariane.

"Yes," answer all the children in unison.

"In this great country, which fought for such beautiful causes as women's rights, freedom, and equality, many people believed for a long time that men and women with black skin, like me, were intellectually inferior, less hard-working and carriers of diseases," Ariane tells them slowly.

A little boy vigorously shakes his hand.

"But how is that possible? It doesn't make sense. People are all the same. If there are biological differences, they are negligible. It has certainly nothing to do with skin color. In fact, twenty thousand years ago, everyone had black skin. How could people of the United States, who should have known better, think that?" he asks her in return.

Tabitha tells herself that her mother, if it wasn't by coincidence, had definitely chosen a class with children with high potential, and this boy would one day surely join a Medicine Center.

Ariane smiles at him even more and answers him:

"The European people who settled on the continent called North America had white skin. They brought slaves from a continent called Africa and made them work on their farms, which they called plantations. These slaves from Africa had black skin. But as the new Americans needed to justify what was unjustifiable—using people as their own property—they invented stories about how Blacks were different. And even when they abolished slavery, prejudice continued long after. Some even created what were called 'Jim Crow' laws to maintain this racial order. For example, in some cities, black children and white children could not attend the same schools."

Ariane pauses for a moment, lost in pre-war history, probably trying to formulate her ideas as simply and clearly as possible.

"The myths that people believe are called Culture. And do you children know what we in the Red World believe about skin color?" asks Ariane in a cheerful and positive voice.

A little blonde girl answers in a soft voice:

"There is no racism in the Red World because we base ourselves only on knowledge and facts. And above all, we desire peace."

Ariane applauds with pleasure, stands up to show she is leaving, and exits the class, followed by Tabitha, under the admiring eyes of the children. They will remember clearly this exceptional moment when they met some Elites.

The mother and daughter go back towards the exit, still passing through immaculate white corridors, where the sounds of their fast footsteps echo noisily.

As they are still alone, Ariane takes the opportunity to tell her:

"A hundred years ago, Tabitha, the Founders created our society to try to retain the best of Humanity. Our ancestors had destroyed everything: nature, animals, entire populations, after centuries and centuries of wars, unimaginable violence, and horrors. Our world has now lived in peace for a hundred years. You and I in the Red World are not judged by the color of our skin. We are Ariane and Tabitha, Elites."

Ariane stops and stares at Tabitha with an intense look.

"What you're doing right now, the Eight, think about the impact," she continues.

Tabitha is about to respond when several soldiers join them to escort them to Ariane's shuttle.

The two women arrive at the car. When they are both sitting alone, Tabitha can at last tell her. "Mom, you know me, there's no problem. The other seven and I have things under control, but still, I have a request. You see, yesterday, Leah, Cathy, and James..."

Her mother cuts her off.

"This time—and this will definitely be the last time—we will pretend to believe your story about the soldiers killed by Rebels. But from now on, you really need to control yourself. And grow up!"

Then she starts up her flying car, leaving Tabitha speechless.

CHAPTER 5

CHRIS

JUST AS HE IS getting back on the train with his friends, Chris gets a message on his receiver, which might have seemed insignificant to the uninformed eye. Yet Chris knows the real sender and the urgency of the message. He quickly jumps back onto the platform.

"I forgot some things at your mother's, Cathy," he says to them in a tone they all understand.

He runs away fast.

Chris is not very tall. He has slightly brown skin and straight black hair that falls on his glasses, when he chooses to wear them, which makes him look serious. And as soon as he smiles, the softness of his face is contagious.

When he concentrates, his determination and mental strength show through. When he starts to speak, his rather hoarse voice immediately inspires respect. He has the gift of choosing each of his words and everyone ends up listening to him.

Above all, he radiates righteousness, a strong sense of ethics, which makes him one of the most respected among the Eight.

He's only eighteen. Yet few engineers in the Red World have as much knowledge of electronics as he does.

It is for all this, and also for his computer skills, that a group of hackers close to the Rebels hiding in Obama contacted him. The one who just wrote him is a hacker named Zeus—a name that may seem quite pretentious. But when you know that the Red Army has been tracking him for years and has made him one of the most actively-sought Rebels, his choice of the name of an ancient God no longer seems so arrogant. For a long time, he has operated from inside Kantas City, hidden under the identity of a common nobody, similar to so many others in this neighborhood, with their worn-out clothes, sitting on the street or in makeshift shelters, badly fed and mistreated.

Chris stops by Cathy's mom's house to leave his transmitter and change his clothes. The door is open as always. Who would dare venture into her home? This would invite swift retaliation on the part of Cathy and the other Elites.

Chris finds her sitting in front of her window, looking out, rocking with her usual gentle motion. He has always been Cathy's mother's favorite because of his specific aura, and that's why when she turns around she gives him a great smile, which gives Chris a glimpse of the beauty she had once been. Like each of the Eight who have one or more gifts, Chris can see the auras around people; this morning she has a light green color around her, a sign of a deep healing.

"Chris, there you are! I knew you were coming back. It's good to see you again."

"Mother, I'm leaving for an urgent appointment. Can I leave my transmitter with you as usual?" replies Chris. He is intrigued by her remark, but bites his tongue so as to not ask her what she meant by "I knew."

Cathy's mother remains a mystery for everyone: for the Elites, the Government, and even for Cathy.

"You will soon discover so many things," she says staring at him with a very intense gaze that he has never seen on her before.

For a moment, he imagines her years before, when she was an engineer in nuclear physics, one of the most talented people of her generation. Cathy had told them her story, but he had also heard another version from his own parents. They had told him that if she had not been selected as an Elite, it was only because she did not have the Mark. For what other reason could there be? Her skills were exceptional. Her rise in the hierarchy of the Science Centers had been as spectacular as her fall. The torture she had suffered had destroyed much of her mind and her physical capacity.

Chris can't hide his surprise when she adds:

"Go to Zeus. He, too, is coming close to the truth."

She smiles at him, turns toward the window and resumes her gentle rocking motion.

Chris stands still for a few minutes, trying to understand what she has just said.

Did Zeus come by? Are her gifts coming back after all these years? Or was she, in fact, a Rebel as the Government had thought? He turns these questions over and over in his head, looking for elements of the past that could bring him an answer, while he discreetly sneaks his way onto Obama's streets. Here, the streets are not like in the other districts of Kantas City, where at this time the Actives go to their occupations in the various Centers. Here there is nothing to do, except to hang around in groups and wait for the garbage containers coming from the other districts, to hunt for food in the meager remains.

Chris, isolated, without his Elite uniform and with his small size, could become easy prey. Fortunately, he is carrying one of his toys, a human activity detector, which allows him to sneak around the neighborhood avoiding its dangers. He also runs very, very fast. Today, however, his vertigo has returned, and he feels he is walking on a tightrope. Even as a child he often fell. His parents, unlike most of his friends, had always been very loving and concerned about the welfare of their precocious son. Highly educated, both renowned scientists in the Red World, his parents had quickly noticed their son's physical and mental shortcomings and had taught him how to control his emotions and body. His mother trained him for hours in meditation, and his father spent days and nights passing on all his genetic and electronic knowledge. They assembled and then reassembled all the available machines around them. And Chris especially loved going where they worked. "One day, you will be the leader of the Science Centers," his mother told him. They were so proud when Chris joined the new class of Elite Students.

Chris finally stops in front of the place he's looking for.

"Now, find the box," he tells himself aloud.

He quickly spots a stone near the entrance to the building that looks slightly different. Behind is the famous box where he quickly types his personal code that will give Zeus the signal that it is really he. A man in his thirties immediately comes out and signals for him to follow him down an alley. Finally, after passing through several places, they both find themselves in a dark room in the basement. There are cards and posters on the walls and screens on top of each other. A real mess and a musty smell complete the picture.

Several men and women in their twenties are sitting behind computer screens. They all seem to come from different backgrounds, not just from the Obama neighborhood.

Chris is in an actual Rebel's nest.

He removes the hood that completely covered his face. Everyone looks at him with the usual mixture of respect and fear in their eyes. Chris also spots anger through his vision of the colors that emanate from them. Zeus' decision to take him to one of their hiding places is not to everyone's liking—which he can fully understand. The Eight are in fact training to become the leaders of the Red World Government, the same Government they fight every day, risking their lives and the lives of their families. Because having a Rebel in a family can mean the worst reprisals for everyone.

Zeus walks towards Chris. He is tall, in his forties, and looks like a man who sleeps on the street, with his unkempt hair and badly trimmed beard. The two men hug. Since they met two years ago, they have become like father and son.

"It feels good to see you, Chris," he says, holding him.

"Likewise, Zeus, likewise," replies Chris.

“t’s really good of you to come here because a lot of weird things are going on,” he says worriedly, while dragging Chris to his workstation.

“First of all, are you young people aware of the potential food rationing and the plan to expel from the Dome or even kill a lot of people this time?” asks Zeus.

“Yeah, we heard the rumor yesterday. It seems they need to go from 100,000 to 80,000. Are those the numbers you have too?”

“Yeah, that’s what we found.”

“We also managed to get into one of the computers of one of the big bosses of Strategies. They’re running simulations and scenarios at full speed,” Chris adds.

Zeus looks straight ahead, then at all his friends around him.

“Chris, if this really happens, it’ll blow everything up, you know that?”

Chris nods and encourages him to go on.

“We are almost ready,” Zeus says in a determined voice.

His eyes now seem filled with fire at the thought of a possible imminent revolution.

The other Rebels hang onto his words. They, too, are waiting for what Zeus will say next.

“Chris, I called you especially because we have detected three new centers of human activity.”

While giving him this information, he shows him a screen with the geographical locations that Chris memorizes immediately. The three centers are at various distances, two very far and one at 300 kilometers from the Dome.

“This is the one your friends visited yesterday.”

“How do you know that, Zeus?”

"Because I am Zeus, of course," he replies with a hearty laugh. "Well, I do know Noah well. You know, the pilot?"

Chris is about to answer him when Zeus looks at him strangely. Then suddenly he takes him in his arms, hugging him even harder than a few minutes before.

"Chris, I have faith in you and your friends. It's very important that you understand what's going on in the world. Here, in the Red World, and elsewhere. Please leave quickly. There's no time to waste."

At this, Zeus turns around, signaling the end of their conversation. But then Chris sees an aura of sadness, a very gray color, emerging around him. He then leaves as quickly as possible; he has to find his friends.

CHAPTER 6

STEPHANIE

STEPHANIE WATCHES CHRIS GET off the train and head back to Obama. She can't help feeling a knot in her stomach at the thought of him going to Obama district by himself. Of course, Chris is like all of them, very well trained. But still, she's worried.

"Come on, Stephanie! Your lover will be fine without you," Jesse says.

Stephanie moves as if to deliver an uppercut to Jesse's jaw.

"Stop talking nonsense like you always do," Leah tells him. Leah grabs Stephanie's hand, very discreetly, and holds her tightly for a few seconds.

James intervenes then, but this time telepathically:

"Still, maybe I should have gone with him this time."

"James, you can't always be a bodyguard or even a babysitter for everyone," says Jesse. *"We have to be able to get our act together by ourselves."*

Max adds:

"Jesse's right this time. James, you can't always be there to protect us. Still, he seemed absolutely worried this time. Something in the way he is walking. Haven't you noticed he's been limping a little lately?"

Stephanie can't believe her senses.

"Max, please stop. Don't get into it too! It's true that even if it's not rational, I don't like him going alone."

Jesse intervenes:

"You guys are making up stories right now. Chris is fine. Stephanie, you are not being rational. There is no, absolutely no, scenario in which Chris could be in danger in Obama. He has all the technological and physical tools, as well as his gifts, to get out of any situation. Besides, nobody can run as fast as he."

"Thank you, Jesse," answers Stephanie. And her thanks is sincere.

Jesse mumbles "You're welcome," then turns his head.

Meanwhile, Stephanie's train continues its journey through the nearly identical square or rectangular buildings. They are crossing the Pluto district where the office towers of the Strategy Centers are located and where live the privileged Actives of the Medicine and Strategy Centers. A smile appears on Stephanie's face. She loves this neighborhood so much. It's where she grew up and where her dear parents still live. Like Chris, she had a happy childhood being both spoiled and admired. Both Doctors of Medicine, her parents had done everything to develop her potential to the maximum, bestowing her with books and information. "Unfortunately for me, they failed to see the violent aspect of the program," she murmurs.

A memory suddenly pops into her head. She is eight years old. It is her first day as an Elite student and some instructors took her and her classmates to a combat training room. An instructor asks Jesse to fight Max and he knocks Max out in record time. Then that same instructor asks her to fight Chris. She looks at Chris and sees only the softness behind his eyes and cannot raise her fist. Chris is also helpless, not knowing what to do. They bring Jesse back on the mat to teach Chris a lesson.

The train's arrival at the Elite station brings to an end this painful memory.

When the Elite students get off the train, the other passengers get out of the way to let them pass. They then begin to run quickly towards their training building. It is a huge structure, a large white bunker, recognizable by the red line surrounding the building, symbol of the Red World as well as their Elite Unit. When they were little, they didn't understand how that entire building would be made only for them, the Eight. Little by little, they had used every room and explored every nook and cranny—the gym, combat training, martial arts, education center, their own library, the physical recovery center, the two swimming pools, the climbing walls where they learned to climb like insects, and finally the artificial forest—all of this under the supervision of controllers, trainers, programmers, engineers, and educators. Dozens of employees dedicated to the successful completion of their training. Not to mention the steady stream of soldiers sent to sacrifice themselves for their training needs. And of course, there was their little Kitchen, their cloakroom and their dormitory, all three tiny. Indeed, most of the space was allocated to their development, if not to their well-being.

Stephanie has booked time in the library during her activity program. She wants to research the train station that Leah, Cathy, and James discovered. Now she regrets her choice. The others go together to the pool to do lengths, daily exercise for their physical fitness, and she would have loved to have gone with them if only to avoid being alone with her anxieties. To calm herself, she starts to perfectly arrange everything she finds in front of her. "Another thing I share with Chris," she says with a smile. In the morning, they can each be seen meticulously tidying their beds and things.

Sitting in front of a computer, instead of looking for information about the station, she finds herself typing "Anna Karenina." The first line of the book appears: "All happy families are alike; each unhappy family is unhappy in its own way."

Stephanie has a special gift: a photographic memory, one that has yet to find any limits. For ten years, she has been gradually absorbing all the knowledge available in the center, and thus in all of Kantas City. That makes her a walking computer. Naturally, she is fascinated by everything that is not factual, including love and the strange feelings she has for Chris. Tolstoy and Anna Karenina confuse her and she often plunges back into this book to find answers to her questions.

As she resumes her reading, an instructor enters the room. It is Doctor M. He is often assigned to Cathy's training, which is why Stephanie is surprised to see him. But she remembers that Cathy trusts him completely and relaxes quickly.

Doctor M sits in front of her.

"What do you think about love, Stephanie?"

Stephanie is surprised by this question, because love is never a subject they discuss in the Red World. But their training is often full of surprises. Stephanie replies, repeating what she learnt, "Love has been history's greatest cause of war, crime, and misery. Literary romanticism is only a myth to make the human condition bearable. Humans have been slaves since the agricultural revolution ten thousand years ago. Slaves to their condition, their desires, and to consumerism, before the Ecological Wars."

"And what do you think..." he pauses, clearing his throat, "... of intimate relations between two people?"

"Everyone is free to do what they want and with whom they want. But this must above all serve procreation, obviously limited for the benefit of the community. Many women have suffered since time immemorial from sexual enslavement, humiliation, and rape. Any sexual predator must be immediately eliminated from the Red World."

"Good answer, Stephanie. And now I'm going to activate my signal jammer, as you see me doing here. And I'll ask you again," he adds with a big smile.

Stephanie looks at him doubtfully. Doctor M is a tall man with a sullen face. He wears round glasses and has a peculiar way of walking. His back is a little arched. He's losing his hair and must be nearly fifty. In short, he doesn't look very important. Yet not only is he a Doctor, which is the highest distinction, but according to Cathy he is far above the standard of the other educators.

"How do I know you're not testing me right now?"

"Let's just say, right now, your boyfriend Chris is meeting a hacker named Zeus. The latter will provide him with essential information for your next days. And a pilot named Noah accompanied your friends yesterday. So, I ask you again. There is no trap, trust me. What do you think about love?"

Stephanie quickly feels that, first, he must be telling the truth, and second, there is no great risk in answering this question. However, she waits a few seconds before answering him, to digest what she has just heard.

"Okay. What I think is..."

She thinks long and hard.

"Don't hide behind your knowledge. Just tell me how you feel," Doctor M suggests, this time with less patience in his voice.

"Okay. What I feel is a knot in the middle of my stomach whenever he's not near me. My heart gets very tight as soon as I see him get hurt, or when he hasn't noticed that I've entered the room."

Stephanie almost feels relieved to be able to free herself and talk about the feelings she has carefully repressed until now.

"But most of all," she continues, "I feel vulnerable because I am more afraid for his life than for mine, and that bothers me."

"That's good, propaganda doesn't work on you," answers Doctor M. "Love will always be an important motive for you and your survival. We shouldn't believe everything we're told. Love is the most beautiful thing in the world. Most important of all, Stephanie, never show them that because they could use it against you. Love is your weakness."

"Who are *they*?"

"You'll know soon enough."

"Tell me right now, who is this *they*?" she answers angrily.

"The discussion is over, Stephanie. My name is Leo, for the record," he says with a wink.

He deactivates the signal jammer and quickly leaves the room, leaving Stephanie totally stunned.

CHAPTER 7

JAMES

JAMES WATCHES STEPHANIE WALK away towards the library, while the rest of the troupe, now only Max, Cathy, Leah, Jesse, and James, go to the swimming pools.

"She should have come with us," James tells Cathy, who is walking alongside him.

To answer, Cathy raises her shoulders, clearly annoyed.

"What's wrong with you, Cathy? Honestly, you're super weird today!"

"Because you don't think everything's been super weird since yesterday?" she replies in a tight voice.

At that moment, Jesse, walking in front of the four of them, suddenly stops, tripping them all behind him.

"Hey, guys, listen to this! My dearest Father, Master of the World, summons me immediately. He sends me his Government shuttle that arrives in... uh.... two minutes! Well, g'bye guys. Enjoy your bath!"

He runs back to the front door.

Cathy turns around, her arms crossed, to face James.

"Oh, wow. Is that weird or what?"

Leah and Max also look back at them, intrigued by the turn that the conversation is taking.

"Don't take me for an idiot, Cathy. Of course, there are strange things going on. Look, there's only the four of us left. We always use to be together. But there's no need to take it out on me," he says with a sad look.

Max intervenes in the conversation.

"Hey guys, calm down, okay? We're all going to the swimming pools—well, what remains of our group. We'll relax and then we'll meet in the Kitchen to discuss all of this together."

"Wow, Max, you're becoming a real leader, aren't you?" says Leah teasingly.

"Right. Don't you start too," he replies with mock anger.

He takes her by the hand and runs with her towards the swimming pool.

Cathy looks at James, jumps to kiss him, and then runs after Leah and Max.

James pauses for a few seconds, still surprised by this mark of affection. He gently touches his cheek, where Cathy kissed him, then follows them towards his pool.

Yes, his pool.

Even after years spent in the Center, he is still surprised that the Government has built him his own swimming pool. They changed the structure of the entire building to accommodate a pool with one lane four times the length of the other pool.

While getting ready in the locker room, James thinks of his parents—those two simple and insignificant beings called A1744 and A8911. Unlike Jesse and Tabitha, who from their early childhood had benefited from advantages due to their parents' rank, or even Cathy who had had an exceptional mother in her time.

A1744 and A8911 were anything but exceptional.

A year before James was born, his mother had given birth to a tiny little girl. The child had come out of her mother's womb with a tiny scream and then calmly looked at the world around her before curling up against her mother's breast. James' parents were Actives in the Administration, both in lower positions. They wanted no more than a simple and predictable life in their very small house in the Saturn district. The arrival of this little girl, who seemed very wise, foreshadowed beautiful years for the three of them before she herself would one day became an Active and leave the home.

The first few weeks were wonderful. The little girl's gurgling brightened their small two-bedroom house. She ate, slept, and discovered the world in the arms of her beloved parents. The mother stayed at home for a whole day, then the next day it was the father's turn, as the Founders had decreed at the beginning of the Red World. They were eager to take turns staying with her so they could go to the park, give her milk rations, specially prepared for her and provided daily by the Medical Unit, and cuddle her at home. Every Sunday they attended a class with other parents from the Administration Centers, to help each other and share their problems as new parents. This group would become a great source of support and friendship for years to come. The children would be friends and would go to the same Education Center. A1744 and A8911 were very happy and proud.

Then on the thirtieth day after her birth, the sweet little girl, with her big blue eyes, did not wake up. The mother's wails of horror echoed for several minutes throughout the neighborhood. A team from the Medical Unit quickly arrived on the scene and took the child away.

Their grief was immeasurable.

Under Red World rules, only one child was allowed per family. The rule was strict, but there were a few exceptions. If a child died before the first month, parents were given permission to have another.

Soon James' mother was pregnant again. This time, her pregnancy went very differently from the start. She had very severe pain all day long, was ravenous and often had to eat her partner's ration. She would wake up some mornings with bruises on her stomach because the child had been kicking. At seven months pregnant, A1744 was so much bigger than at the same time with the little girl. The doctors decided not to wait and to operate immediately to take out the baby. It was a boy twice the size of the baby girl, who screamed so loudly that everyone on the floor heard him and some even rushed to the room where he had been delivered from his mother's womb. The doctors took turns observing the baby and decided to quickly take him out of sight of his parents and keep him for observation.

A1744 and A8911 were inconsolable. Not only was their beloved little girl dead, but now their son, whom they barely had time to see, was taken from them. After that, a member of the Government came to see them every week to reassure them that their son was fine.

Then one morning, eight months after his birth, the Government decided to take James back to his parents to be raised there for his first eight years.

James is now approaching the pool. The sight of water is irresistible to him and a dose of adrenaline rushes through his body. He dives in and lets the cold numb his muscles for a few seconds before he starts his movements and lets all his power explode.

He thinks about Jesse and his father. When you are Aldo, one of the most brilliant Elite students in history and now a member of the Government in charge of the Army, you obviously expect your only child, in this case Jesse, to have been born extraordinary. But when you're A1744 and A8911, and a Government shuttle brings your eight-month-old baby back to you, and the baby is already walking and as big as a two-year-old, you don't have the same reaction. James remembers his mother's face at that moment, an expression of horror and disgust. With this in mind, James accelerates his swimming and finds himself at the end of the pool in just a few breaststrokes.

"It's funny how an image can remain engraved in your memory and still hurt you so much," James reflects. Unfortunately, this does not ease his sadness.

A1744 and A8911 had done their best to raise James. But he was so strong that he often broke everything around him without wanting to. In the park, the other children were afraid to play with him.

James felt his parents' embarrassment. The first time his father saw him stay underwater for several minutes, he cried for his neighbors, thinking the little boy was dead. Or when James figured out how to move water from one glass to another using just the strength of his mind, his mother dropped the plate she was holding. When he was taken away at the age of eight to become an Elite student, James didn't have to be a telepath to sense their relief.

Since then, on the rare occasions when the three of them met, an embarrassed silence dropped between them. Because above all, A1744 and A8911 really didn't understand how they could have given life to a child with the Mark.

CHAPTER 8

JESSE

JESSE RUNS TO THE exit where his father's flying car must be waiting for him. If he has to go see Aldo, which he doesn't enjoy, at least he gets to fly in his father's shuttle. Jesse finds this exhilarating. One of Aldo's security guards is already waiting for him in front of the shuttle.

"Hello, Jesse. Aldo sent me to come with you. Shall I go up first?"

"No, I'm going up!" replies Jesse who boards the shuttle in two hops and closes the door quickly.

The guard looks at him a little bewildered, then quickly hits his radio to alert his boss. Aldo will undoubtedly be furious, which adds to Jesse's pleasure to be alone in this superb machine. Of course, Jesse loves to fly and he shares this passion with Tabitha; it is the privilege of their upbringing. He takes the opportunity to fly above the different districts. He goes up to the top of the Dome to get an overview. Everything seems so organized, except in the Obama district of course. Jesse often wonders why the Founders created it and why the current Government still tolerates it. Maybe to remind others of what their lives could be like if they don't follow the rules? He plunges down in a dive as fast as possible to reach the main Army Center. He parks on the roof where there is direct access to Aldo's office. Several guards are waiting to escort him. Jesse gets out of the shuttle and follows them without a word, just with his usual smirk. Like all the Eight, he doesn't like the military very much and finds their main center utterly repulsive. According to Cathy, there are rumors in Obama of experiments on local men and women caught in raids. Every time he comes to this place, Jesse cannot help but wonder how the Army Centers will change under James' leadership—because James is so good. On the other hand, he will first have to spend a few years under Aldo's authority to receive his training, and that can change a man.

The main Army Center is one of the highest building in Kantas City and Aldo's office is naturally at the top, overlooking the city. Aldo is actually looking out and tells him without turning back:

"I watched your flying. You still have some progress to make."

"All you have to do is lend me your toy more often," Jesse replies.

Aldo turns around to look at his son. They don't see each other very often, and he can't help but notice once again how much his son looks like his mother. He has the same slender appearance, arrogant posture, jet-black hair, rawboned features, almost gray-blue eyes that reflect a very real coldness. Certainly, the perfect beauty combined with his wife's calculating coldness had strongly attracted Aldo at first. But he soon paid the price.

Jesse looks at him and thinks exactly the same thing. How can this man be his father? Aldo is tall, strong and bulky. Yes, bulky. To his enormous muscle mass a touch of fat has been added. Stephanie says that he looks like an old Viking. He is blond, hot-tempered, with a thundering voice and a mood that can change in a few seconds from a loud and contagious joy to an anger so strong that the violence exhibited distorts his features—making him extremely threatening.

"You know, Jesse, this is going to happen soon. You're going to be able to use the shuttles. You'll soon stop playing like a kid and come join the grown-ups."

"Because you had fun there at the Training Center?"

"Way more than today!" Aldo replies without skipping a beat.

"Well, the idea to start the training in the Operation Centers sounds exciting," Jesse says teasingly.

"Honestly, Jesse, I don't know if it's your Elite class that's—How do I put it? —immature and stupid?" Aldo laughs with a loud guffaw.

Jesse shrugs off his father's remark.

"Is that what you in the Government think of us? That we're stupid? Is that why you summoned me, like Ariane who's with Tabitha right now?"

"Do you know what they are both talking about?"

Jesse hears the concern in Aldo's question.

"No, she's still with her. What's going on, Dad?"

Aldo jumps when he hears this last word. It is so rare that his son calls him *Dad.*

Aldo is still wondering what he's going to say to Jesse about the meeting they had last night. Besides, now he knows that the manipulative Ariane called to meet her daughter this morning. Aldo remembers her as she was last night, sublime and haughty as usual.

Aldo and the others had been meeting in the Government command room. They had left the Elite Training Center Kitchen a long time ago, and yet, out of habit, they always sat in the same places. An atmosphere similar to the one in which they lived in the Training Center settled almost immediately, eight in a ring wondering who was going to take control.

Ariane, this time, is the first to open fire.

"So, after what happened this afternoon, you still want to let them out? Six soldiers shot down? And not the weak ones."

Ariane adds, looking straight into the eyes of her colleague in front of her: "Except if Aldo, who, as we all know, has become feeble, has also weakened his soldiers."

Aldo is very close to losing his cool and rising to the bait but finally comes to his senses.

"It's a very simplistic vision, uncharacteristic of you, by the way. They're just very strong. Especially this Cathy," replies Aldo.

Nils, in charge of the Strategy Center, speaks in a biting and mocking voice. "There you go! There you go, that Cathy again. Is that your poor excuse?"

"I didn't say that, Nils. I'm just saying they're very strong. And maybe even more than you all think. This is crazy. Am I the only one who can see clearly here?"

Rose, a small, redheaded woman in charge of Medicine, looks at him while shaking her head.

"That's because Monsieur has his son in the Elite class. So, certainly, the Elite students are very strong. And it was your guys who were killed, wasn't it? Maybe you're the one who can't see very clearly here."

Aldo shakes his head and crosses his arms, like a petulant child.

Nils intervenes:

"We said we would let them out, but I have my doubts too."

"So now you're starting to do it too? What is it this time? They're in cahoots with the Rebels, aren't they?" adds Rose as she begins to laugh.

"Don't talk to me like that, Rose. Yes, I continue to receive information and I think it should be taken very seriously," Nils says in his solemn tone.

"My daughter in contact with Rebels!" replies Ariane, laughing in turn. "You're kidding, Nils. I already told you, this is bullshit. You don't look any more in control of your spies than poor Aldo does of his soldiers. Tabitha hates the Rebels and anything that would question her status as an Elite."

"It's true it's hard to imagine, knowing your daughter. She is so arrogant," Rose adds, looking to the sky.

"And you, Aldo, what do you think of your beloved son having fun with the Rebels?" asks a medium-sized man named Ajay.

"Hmm. Jesse is so twisted. And there's Cathy in the group. Remember who she is. Matilda, what do you think?" Aldo asks, turning to a tall blonde with a gray and cold stare.

Matilda is in charge of Justice and often serves as peacemaker in their conflicts. Like the others, Aldo is suspicious of her, but he admits that she is often right.

"I understand your concerns," she says. "But it's no use. We have to follow the plan, like our elders before us. So, Nils, until you have tangible evidence to give us, everything you say is pure speculation and has no value."

Nils gives her a murderous look.

"My turn," says Megan, a tiny little woman with formidable intelligence, in charge of the Arts and Nature Center. "Matilda is right, as always. We have to follow the plan even if they are stronger than we think, an improved new generation of Elites. Exciting, isn't it? Even if they are in contact with the Rebels. And maybe Cathy is, indeed, the disruptive element."

"The propaganda we spread must not work on them," says Ajay. "But then, it didn't work on us either," he adds with a big smile.

"That's for sure," says Ariane. "You would have been nicer to have around."

"And also, less stupid," Rose adds.

Ajay looks at them, shaking his head. "Let them say what they want, these bitches."

Glen, a slim, tall, sharp-eyed man, who still hasn't said a word but whose presence alone fills the room, finally intervenes:

"Of course, Matilda is right. It really doesn't matter whether they are a weaker or stronger class than us, whether they are attracted or not by Rebel theories. Even if they are in contact with them, it is obvious that this will have very interesting consequences for us to follow."

Matilda adds, "Going out is part of their initiation. That's all there is to it. The Founders wanted it that way."

"We must also recognize that the world has changed a lot since then and that this is an experience that can be very painful," reflects Glen.

He pauses and everyone is lost in thought, and their silence says a lot about the hardships they already went through.

"But they have to go through this, whatever the consequences," Glen adds.

"Let's vote then," offers Matilda.

They all look at each other. The strong animosity that had prevailed until then has vanished. They have become united again by the most difficult trial they have ever had to face together, where their true personalities and courage have been put to the test. The young Elite students will have to face this in turn. Soberly, they all raise their hands.

<u>Government Organization Chart</u>

Aldo - Army	Rose - Medicine
Nils - Strategy	Ariane - Education
Ajay - Administration	Megan - Arts and Nature
Glen - Science	Matilda - Justice

Aldo comes out of his thoughts and looks at his son. It's true that he doesn't look like him and that they never really had any chemistry, but he's still his son. And it was a miracle that they all came out of it alive twenty-five years ago.

Glen is right. The world has changed a lot since the Founders established this rule for Elite learning. His teams and the spies who have recently left Kantas City have all confirmed it.

"What's the matter, Dad?" Jesse asks again, puzzled by Aldo's silence and apparent nervousness.

"I certainly wasn't the best father," says Aldo. "But I called you here just to give you some advice. Here it is. You will experience the most difficult trial of your training. Please don't underestimate it. And stay close to Tabitha. That's all. That's all."

Aldo turns around and looks outside again, the way he was when Jesse walked into his office. Jesse notices that his father now has a slightly arched back. Jesse decides to send him one last bombshell to see how he will react.

"During the trial, as you call it, remember: if you touch Mom, I will kill you."

Jesse is waiting for a reaction that doesn't come, but he suspects that Aldo's posture has sunk a little further.

Surprised, he very quickly leaves his father to find his friends. He climbs with great strides up the stairs that bring him back to the roof. The flying car is still there. He rushes up inside and doesn't bother this time to fly over Kantas City. He lands in front of the Training Center and runs in the corridors towards the pools.

"Come on, get out, guys! It's urgent. In the Kitchen, right now."

Leah, Cathy, and James jump out of the pool and rush to the locker room.

Jesse then goes to pick up Stephanie and both rush to the Kitchen, joined by Chris and Tabitha. Leah, James, Cathy, and Max arrive a few seconds after them.

CHAPTER 9

CATHY AND THE EIGHT

CATHY TRIES TO SLOW down the beating of her heart while she puts her clothes on. She breathes gently, focusing on a point in the room, and tries to calm her mind. But deep down, she feels that something extraordinary is finally going to happen. First, there had been her mother's behavior with her this morning. She seemed so happy, serene, and above all, awake. Her mother never talked about the torture she and her husband had suffered. But Cathy had seen the scars that crisscrossed her body. On top of that, her beloved father had succumbed to his wounds. Cathy was six years old then. They lived in a very beautiful house in the Uranus district. They were both Doctors, researchers in nuclear physics and among the most brilliant citizens of the Red World. Cathy had felt their absence for several weeks. She had been taken to an orphan center, where she had spent her time fighting against the other children who treated her like a leper. Some time later, her mother had returned home alone. She was just a shadow of her former self. The next day, they moved to a new apartment in Obama, where she still lives.

The unexpected serenity of her dear mother had warmed her heart. *Something's going to happen, that's for sure. Something very important, and probably related to my mother,* she says to herself as she enters the Kitchen with her friends.

Chris, Jesse, Tabitha, and Stephanie are already there, just recently because they, too, are out of breath.

Chris is standing there fidgeting on the spot. "Ah, there you are at last! All right, no need to continue telepathically, folks. I've activated the signal jammer. We can talk freely."

Chris seems so excited that none of them think of interrupting him. Cathy thinks he suddenly looks so young, like a fourteen-year-old boy. But if Chris takes such risks using his jammer in the Center, it must be very important.

"Something strange happened, Cathy. Your mother knew about my meeting with Zeus."

Cathy can't help but shudder. "What?" she exclaims.

"Chris, were you with Zeus?" Stephanie intervenes. "Do you know how dangerous that is?"

"You shouldn't have gone there without us discussing it," Tabitha adds. "I don't agree with this. You put us all in danger."

"It's kind of cool, Cathy. So, your mother also knows Zeus?" says Jesse, giving her a mocking wink.

"Jesse, stop it!" Max intervenes. "Give her a break."

Leah approaches Cathy and asks her the question that everyone has on their lips:

"Cathy, do you think your parents were really Rebels?" she asks her in a calm and gentle voice.

"Of course not!" replies Cathy in a strident tone. "I would have told you, obviously. I know that this is what the Government thought then, and I see how everyone looks at me. But it's not true!"

Tabitha intervenes.

"Obviously it must be a shock to you, Cathy, but excuse me, that's not the most important thing right now. Please continue your story, Chris," she says in an authoritative voice.

Cathy makes an effort to keep calm and stay focused.

"I went to my appointment with Zeus, and to make a long story short, I found myself in a room with about ten Rebels—some hackers, from all over Kantas City. That Zeus exposed himself in this way is totally incomprehensible to me. They were all very nervous to see me there. In short, he gave me three locations of human activities outside the Dome and left me as if he would never see me again. I didn't understand anything."

"Locations, why?" asks Stephanie.

"I don't know," Chris replies. "I told you. I didn't understand anything. Oh, I forgot, he also knew about yesterday's getaway."

"The Rebel pilot Noah who was with us, did he talk about it?" asks James.

"Yeah, he knew him. It's crazy, isn't it?" Chris replies.

"Perhaps my father is right to be nervous and to say that there are more and more Rebel activities. Perhaps even within the

Government. And maybe the Government also thinks, rightly, that we are in contact with them," Jesse adds.

"My mother also behaved strangely this morning," says Tabitha. "We didn't even have a proper conversation. She just took me to visit one of her Centers and spent all the time bragging about the benefits of being part of the Red World. She used the angle of racism against black people. Can you believe it? She must be pretty worried to behave that way."

As Tabitha says this last sentence, she gives Chris an insistent look.

"I know what it is," Stephanie says with a smile. "It's our last trial!"

At that moment, an announcement is heard in their Kitchen: "Elite students must go immediately to the entrance of the Building."

"Here we go, guys, here we go," says Jesse.

Cathy feels the excitement throughout her body and starts running with her friends.

Upon their arrival in front of the building, a shuttle awaits them and transports them within minutes to the northern entrance of the Dome, where about twenty armed soldiers surround the Eight Leaders in charge of the Government.

Cathy and her friends get out of their shuttle and move towards them. The members of the Government are wearing their official uniforms. The Eight Young Elites stand in front of them. Only twenty-five years separate them, yet it seems to be centuries.

Nils, head of the Strategy Centers and a very influential member of the group, takes the floor.

"My dear Elite students. You are about to commence a crucial trial of your training, which will allow you to rise to the level required to one day join the Red World Government. Behind you is a shuttle especially prepared for you with food and equipment for your journey. Your flight plan is already programmed. You're going to leave now and you'll have to get back in exactly ten days. Not a day more, not a day less. Another rule: all eight of you must come back or the door won't open."

The eight friends look at each other, surprised by this last condition.

"After that, if you succeed, you will integrate into your respective Units where you will begin your training as a future leader.

The Eight Government leaders make their exit, surrounded by their guards, without a glance or an additional word for the young Elites.

Cathy and her friends walk towards the entrance and discover a state-of-the-art shuttle. They all look at each other. The excitement is palpable.

"This is the adventure, guys. This is it. The great adventure!" exclaims Max.

PARIS, YEAR 2025 – INDIGO

INDIGO WAKES WITH A start, as she has every night in recent months, and looks at her alarm clock. "Four o'clock in the morning today, my dear Indigo. Come on, a little effort and you'll be able to sleep all night," she says out loud. Her meditation teacher advised her to speak aloud as soon as she wakes up to help her chase away the visceral anguish that engulfs her at night and wakes her. Normally, she would then do ten breathing exercises, focusing on her favorite image, the Bay of Arcachon. Then her belly, tightened by this cold anguish, would relax gently. But today her intuition tells her that something is going to happen. Her anxiety is palpable.

She went to see several psychologists because the lack of sleep was beginning to have a serious impact on the quality of her work. Some said it was as a result of Ben's departure almost a year ago, which left an immeasurable void. Others said that it was because of her job as a television journalist and the news of the world that she has to follow fourteen hours a day. It is true that lately the world is not going well. The

Americans and Russians have resumed their infernal arms race, while the North Koreans, now holders of their own nuclear arsenal, threaten to blow up their neighbors to the south. The United Nations is locked in reforms and watches helplessly as dozens of countries in Africa and the Middle East get caught up in civil wars. The American and Russian oil giants continue to draw resources from the Arctic, despite the interventions of independent environmentalist groups and European countries, and it is only a matter of months before the Gulf Stream goes completely out of control.

"Come on, enough Indigo. It's time to go for a walk and watch Paris sleep." She swiftly puts on a sports outfit that completely covers her slim, athletic body. She ties her long, black, curly hair with an elastic band and sets off at a good pace down the rue Léon Jost. She likes her street and her neighborhood in the 17th arrondissement of Paris and feels at home, but when she leaves this morning, everything seems very different. She notices the streetlights are not lit yet, but there is a light coming from above the buildings. She walks towards the Courcelles metro station, to get to her usual Café. The wind seems colder than in the previous mornings and it seems to her that there is less noise around her. There is a very unusual scent in the air similar to burnt cinnamon. She moves forward quickly, shivering, anxious to find the warmth of her Café where Ernest will serve her a good espresso with a hot croissant just out of the oven. At the end of her street, she enters the rue des Dardanelles, which leads to the rue de Courcelles. Then, what she sees stops her. It is as if a hurricane had just ripped through and swept away the cars, some of which lie upside down. There is no one, just that light coming from above that illuminates the entrance to the Courcelles metro station. "It must be a dream," she tells herself. And suddenly the pain in her left shoulder intensifies. She had been selected to test a new vaccine against the Ebola virus; a virus that was now rampant all over the world, and since then a Mark appeared on

her shoulder blade. She quickly enters her Café: the door is open, yet there is no one there. Despite the darkness, she can clearly see the brass counter, tired from years of use, but witness to so many lives. The ten tables are in their place, including the one in the right-hand corner where she likes to sit and watch passers-by without being seen. She instinctively sits at her usual table, hoping to see Ernest appear and say to her, "Hello, my little lady, always so early in the morning, eh?" But a few minutes pass and Ernest still doesn't come. Suddenly, a man and a woman enter the Café. They are about her age, in their early thirties, and are regulars, like her. They look at her and then gently lift up their shirts to show their shoulders, revealing the same Mark as hers. Then all the anguish subsides. She knows it. She has always known it. Her life will finally begin and her destiny will be fulfilled.

PART 2

OUTSIDE KANTAS CITY - YEAR 2125

CHAPTER 10

DISCOVERING FREEDOM

Day 1 of the trip, year 2125

THE EIGHT ARE IN the shuttle. They look all around them. They've never seen a vessel like this before.

"They've kept their little secret very well," Jesse says.

"Max, look. They even packed musical instruments for you," James says, showing him a closet where there are wind instruments, a kind of piano, and drums. A whole set of equipment that seems to be made especially for him.

"And we have lots to eat," says Tabitha with a big smile, showing them a full cupboard.

"We also have medicines," adds Leah, who has already started to inventory everything that is available.

"Guys! Guys! We'll finally be able to separate," shouts Tabitha excitedly.

Tabitha has also opened two doors onto two small cabins with four bunk beds.

"Yay, Tabitha, I'm not going to hear you snoring anymore!" says Jesse, laughing.

Jesse, for his part, is standing with Cathy in front of another closet that is almost the size of a room, where the weapons are kept. With Cathy, they are inspecting all the equipment: knives, rifles, guns, bombs, ammunition, as well as other gadgets, each looking complex and menacing.

Meanwhile, Chris is with Stephanie looking at all the available data on the computers.

"What's the gear like?" James asks them.

"They have carefully chosen what they want to leave us," Chris replies. "I'm going to have to import a lot of stuff to be able to go exploring."

"Did you find the flight plan?" asks James, settling himself into the cockpit.

"Yes, I have it."

"So?" they all ask in unison.

They all look at each other laughing.

"I know it," says Stephanie.

"Well, Miss I-Know-Everything, can you tell us then?" asks Jesse with a smile.

"If you ask nicely," interjects Chris with a feigned stern look.

"Okay, Smartest Lady in the Red World, can you give us the flight plan?"

"That's better," answers Stephanie. "We will visit the Red World cities, villages, agricultural centers, as well as study the topography, fauna, and flora. In short, everything is perfectly planned so that we can continue our Elite training in all areas of competence. But this time we'll be outside Kantas City, and alone. Isn't that great?"

"I'm not doing that," exclaims Max.

"Excuse me?"

"Yes, you heard me," says Stephanie. "I'm not doing that."

The silence is deafening in the cabin. Stephanie looks around searching for an ally.

"Tabitha, it is important for our training that we follow the program as expected," says Stephanie.

Tabitha does not answer immediately and turns to her friend.

"Jesse, what do you think?" Tabitha asks.

"Freedom, baby, freedom," he replies.

Chris approaches Stephanie and enfolds her with a protective arm.

"We're going to learn a lot more by going out to discover the world, Stephanie. Don't worry about it."

"Stop with the 'don't worry' thing! You're stressing me out even more," Stephanie answers. "I am not convinced that this is the right thing to do."

"I understand her," says Leah. "What exactly are we looking for by not following their plan?"

"We're going to find out what's really going on in the Red World and beyond. We're going to be free, even if only for ten days. We're going to get the answers to our questions," Cathy answers. "Ten days, ten whole days!"

"I'm with you, Cathy," says James.

"Freedom, baby, freedom," repeats Jesse.

Even if there is still a hint of doubt in Tabitha, Leah, and Stephanie, the prospect of freedom makes it vanish. They all look at each other and a big smile appears on their faces.

Freedom.

No controllers monitoring their actions day and night. No specific program for the day, for every week, month and year. The horizon in front of them and no more Dome above them.

"Great! Great! But I have to get my gear sorted," Chris says, cutting their reverie short.

James and Tabitha settle themselves in the cockpit. Max is next to them figuring out how everything works and helping them check the status of the different piloting gauges: energy levels, pressures, altitude, location, everything.

"What distance do you need to be to be able to upload what you want?" James asks Chris.

"Five hundred meters. That should do it."

"Come on, guys, we're going to take off. Hold on tight," James says, winking towards Tabitha.

The two quickly engage all the different controls, and James raises the control column a few centimeters. The shuttle immediately climbs to several hundred meters above the ground. Then by pushing the handle slightly, they make a jump of nearly 500 meters.

"Wow. What a machine! She responds super well," says James enthusiastically.

"It felt like we hardly moved," Max adds.

"Is it all right for you here, Chris, or should I change our position?" asks James.

"I'm trying to figure it out. I may need a little while. They put up some pretty good firewalls."

"Don't worry about that," says Cathy. "We need to find the surveillance cameras."

"I'll see if I can do anything centrally. But, if I can't, we'll have to go one at a time"

"Better to be safe than sorry," says Cathy as she starts to tear down everything she can see.

"You're right, Cathy," James tells him, leaving the cockpit, and doing the same, followed immediately by the others.

Chris laughs when he sees them so busy. He goes back to his business. He's not really surprised by the level of surveillance that has been put in place, between the cameras and the key-loggers on the shuttle's mainframes. He is, however, shocked by the precautions that prevent him from accessing his own data and programs.

"Are you all right, Chris? You seem worried," Stephanie says to him.

"Yes, it's just that I've never had to deal with so many firewalls," he replies.

"Do you want me to help you?"

Chris looks at Stephanie and immediately gives her a big smile. *Dear Stephanie, she's always right,* he thinks. Chris concentrates and puts himself in telepathy mode.

"Guys, I can't do it. It's just amazing the precautions they took. I can almost admire them. Stephanie is right. I need your help. Everyone, go quietly, while continuing to do what you are currently doing. Each of you take a computer. There is one for each of us. In a few minutes when you

are all ready, you will write exactly what I will dictate to you, obviously by telepathy. A simultaneous attack with the power of the Eight, that's what we're going to do."

They continue to converse as if nothing is happening. Some begin researching on their computers. Others start writing down what they find in the different closets. Then suddenly, at Chris' signal, everyone starts typing very quickly what he tells them. After a few minutes of this, Chris exclaims, "Yeah! Yeah! It's done. We're no longer under their supervision. I still need two more minutes to download what I want."

They watch him furiously typing on the keyboard. *Chris is really the best hacker in the Red World,* they all think.

"Yeah!" he shouts again. "James and Tabitha, start quickly, so we can get out of their sight. I'll jam their radar."

A few minutes later, they land about fifty kilometers away.

"Friends, this is it, it's really freedom!" Chris tells them with tears in his eyes.

Jesse bursts out laughing, throwing his head back, and says to them, "I know some people who are going to scream!"

In the Red World command room in Kantas City, Aldo is indeed unleashing one of his characteristic deep roars. "No, that cannot be happening! I warned you! No more surveillance! What are we going to do now? Shall I send some men to stop them?"

"Calm down, Aldo," says Rose in a dry tone. "The teams will re-establish contact very quickly."

Nils is already on the phone with the central surveillance team.

"They just need a few minutes and everything will be fine," Nils tells them. But his voice, always so full of confidence, reveals a hint of concern.

"They are gone," Ariane declares.

Everyone is looking at the central screen. Indeed, the shuttle has disappeared.

Aldo turns to Ariane and perceives the anxiety in her eyes, which he also shares. His suffering quickly gives way to anger.

"Was that your plan all along, Nils? Let them go so that we could keep the power a little longer?" Aldo asks him in a raging tone, pointing at him aggressively.

"What if they don't come back?" asks Ariane.

"That's bullshit. Why shouldn't they come back?" Megan interrupts them. "Because you think it's particularly nice to live outside when they're about to become the leaders of the Red World?"

"I have spies in the four corners of the Red World and much further away," adds Nils.

Rose starts laughing, interrupting their quarrel. "I'm just disappointed," she says. "I would have quite liked to follow their adventures."

Aldo and Ariane look at her with disgust.

The Eight are gathered in the center of the shuttle.

"Well, now what do we do?" asks Max.

"Clearly, I want to go back to where we were yesterday," says Leah. "Please?" she begs in her sweet little voice.

"There are also the other two coordinates Zeus gave me," Chris adds with determination. "He did not give them away by chance and did not take all these risks for nothing. It must be pretty damn important. We have to go."

"We need to explore the remains of the cities from before the Ecological Wars," says Stephanie with excitement.

All her worries evaporate at the prospect of enriching her knowledge.

"There is our Red World. Let's start there," replies Jesse, with an expression indicating that the choice was obvious.

"What do you think, Cathy?" asks James, who has observed that she has remained silent.

Cathy thinks hard. There are so many places to explore, and so little time.

"I would start with a city in the Red World, the closest from here: Toledo. An old friend of my mother's has taken refuge there—or rather, is hiding there. Well, she went there a long time ago. That would be a good first step."

"It's all the more interesting, Cathy, because Toledo was not part of the original program," Stephanie tells her.

"First, we will have to establish an action plan with a strategy," says Tabitha.

"We need a detailed inventory of everything we have and what we lack," adds Leah.

"I have to work on the new flight plan with James," says Chris.

"Okay, folks. We'll be busy for the rest of the day, that's for sure. The adventure will only start tomorrow," mumbles Jesse.

SOMEWHERE IN THE UNITED STATES, YEAR 2022, SARAH.

------------- *Indigo, Paris, 2025*

------------ *Sarah, United States, 2022*

I DON'T KNOW IF YOU'VE ever experienced this feeling before.

I walk down the street, and suddenly I stop and everything happens in slow motion. I can see this little boy crying while a woman, probably his mother, holds him firmly by the hand and purposefully pulls him along with her, the expression on her face closed, surely late for some appointment. I also see this man in a striped gray suit, perfectly cut, holding a telephone to his ear, speaking a language completely incomprehensible to those who are not working in Wall Street, twirling his free arm as if he would conduct an orchestra. And this elderly woman, who walks slowly, looking down, as if the answer to her many problems that have hunched her back over time is written somewhere on the ground.

These men and women go through their lives with the main objective of satisfying their short-term desires. Would it be possible for the children to finally sleep tonight without waking up, and for me to watch this new series with my husband without interruption, *wonders the woman.* Will I get the best bonus this year allowing me to buy the new Porsche, *ponders the man in the striped gray suit.* How am I going to pay for this room tonight and should I call my son to help me out again?

And yet... If they only knew....

But how could they know, and more particularly, how could they understand?

Sometimes I wonder how I could accept it. And then my mind takes me back to that Monday, where everything changed.

I see myself, sitting in the boardroom, as CEO of a large international pharmaceutical company. I was very proud to have reached such an important position, coming from a modest family in the southern United States.

I still see some of my vice-presidents discussing the opportunity to launch a new product for type 2 diabetes, when my faithful secretary enters the room unannounced, contrary to her usual practice. She whispers in my ear that there was a shooting at Linda's high school. One of the kids shot dozens of students and the police are asking me to get there as soon as possible.

All I remember is shock, a black hole. Normally so rational and in permanent control of my emotions, I had nothing but an empty and totally black hole in my mind. Beth took me by the hand to find my chauffeur who drove me to the school. But I don't remember that. My brain only started working again when I saw the ambulances, the police, the crowd, when I heard the screams, but especially when I saw my beloved daughter's blonde hair, among the other children. Why are they covered in blood? Why is Linda lying there on a stretcher, my only child, my beloved daughter, my reason for living?

When they approached me to join their project, to save humanity as they said, I told them, Why not? I have nothing to lose; I have already lost everything.

But does humanity really deserve to be saved?

I look at the little boy and his mother, the man in the gray striped suit, the elderly lady with the hunched back.

If they only knew....

CHAPTER 11

A REBEL'S NEST

Day 2 of the trip, year 2125

THE DESERT IS THE most shielding of ramparts.

They have gone back. While remaining well away from Kantas City, they follow the path that all those rejected from the Dome take—often in vain—to reach the nearest town, about a three days' walk away, yet still part of the Red World: Toledo.

Their shuttle moves slowly because they don't want to miss an inch of the scenery. Around them lies a rocky desert. The sun, despite the early morning hour, already warms the earth and soon it will become a real furnace with temperatures around forty-five degrees Celsius.

From time to time, they spot makeshift shelters. That is when Max and Leah jump out of the shuttle, looking for possible survivors or at least signs of their passage.

On that day, there is only trash from Kantas City, recognizable by the city's gray and red logo. A few pieces of fabric lie scattered. Sometimes, they see the hastily dug graves of lost or damned souls on their way to a new life.

Finally, they arrive in Toledo.

From afar, the city seems to melt into the desert, with its stone buildings colored like the rocks surrounding the city. Up close, they can see light beige fabrics that cover all the buildings. The camouflage has been positioned to protect against excessive sunlight and recurrent sandstorms. Certainly, this is not as effective as the Dome. It makes the difference between the two cities even more striking.

The shuttle is slowly approaching what appears to be the entrance to the city. A battalion of the Red Army awaits them. A few hundred armed men and women serve as a welcoming committee.

The young Elites have prepared themselves by donning all their combat gear. Infrared devices and various weapons complete their equipment. They decided that Jesse and Tabitha would go into the city. Their status as son and daughter of Leaders is still an asset as long as they remain in the Red World. Cathy and James would accompany them: Cathy to try to find her mother's friend and James as the best bodyguard imaginable. The other four would remain behind to guard the shuttle. It would be a bad idea to lose it on the very first day!

The shuttle lands very close to the troops.

Tabitha comes out first. They decided that there was no point in hiding. In her Elite outfit, with the latest weapons, she advances with confidence towards the man who appears from his uniform to be the Battalion Commander. As always, a palpable tension surrounds her. It is true that the "Princess" is magnificent.

Everyone watches Tabitha, barely noticing Jesse following her. Cathy and James stay back near the shuttle.

"Hello, dear Tabitha. And welcome to Toledo," says the Battalion Commander, a friendly little man with a loud voice.

"Are you waiting for someone?" she asks, falsely surprised, pointing to the army around her.

"We heard that you might come our way and all this is the least we could do to welcome such prominent visitors," he says, bowing slightly.

Tabitha looks at him with disdain.

Jesse is speaking:

"Thank you, Commander. Your good efforts will be widely praised in Kantas City. We would like to visit the town. Would you be so kind as to guide us, or at least give us some indications for the success of our enterprise?"

"All Eight of you?"

"We thought just the four of us," Jesse replies, waving Cathy and James over.

As they move forward, the admiration created by Tabitha's appearance gives way to fear, even hatred. Someone whispers: "Cathy is the daughter of Rebels, and she is part of the Elites!" Someone else adds: "Maybe Cathy is a Rebel!"

Cathy remains perfectly calm, but this only reinforces her determination to understand the history of her parents and the Red World.

The Commander looks at all four of them with curiosity.

"I'll show you the districts that make up this part of the city," he says.

He draws a map in the sand where the Army quarters form a small corner of the square that was supposed to represent the city.

"Apart from this bit," he says, pointing to the rest of the area, "you are alone."

The Commander looks toward Jesse and says with great deference:

"I don't know if you know this, but even with the reinforcements sent by your illustrious father, we have less and less control over this part of the city. We carry out some daily patrols but this is becoming increasingly dangerous for us."

The four Elites look at each other and think the same thing. Aldo is not worried for nothing. The situation is really heating up outside Kantas City.

The Commander signals them to follow him. They cross streets occupied by merchants, soldiers, men and women who seem to come from different parts of the world. The buildings are all gray, white, or black, as in Kantas City. But in Toledo, there is a different atmosphere. There is disarray, but it is much more cheerful. The buildings, despite their color, are more like those in the Obama district and all need repairs. The smell of food mixes with body odors, but this does not bother the four friends at all. On the contrary, for them it is the scent of freedom.

The Commander notes their surprised and curious looks.

“This certainly isn’t Kantas City. I don’t have the same means the Capital has,” he says.

“I like it!” Jesse says, placing one hand on the Commander’s shoulder. “I think you’re doing a great job.”

The Commander relaxes immediately. He has not received a visit from the Government for a long time and the arrival of the young Elites has made him particularly nervous. He admits that since he arrived ten years ago, the city is no longer what it was then. *But hey,* he thinks, *I’m really doing the best I can. If only those damn snobs in Kantas City would give me more resources.*

Jesse and Cathy grin toward each other. Both of them, through their own separate powers, can guess what the Commander is thinking.

Jesse was aware of his gift very early on and took the opportunity to terrorize his little friends in his neighborhood. In class, he would amuse himself by controlling the brains of his teachers who found themselves up to the worst antics—to the general amusement of the children. He could even decide whether or not they would remember the incident. He quite liked that his victims would remember him, the tall skinny guy with straight black hair and ice-colored eyes. The day he joined the Elites, and met Cathy, he immediately tried to get into her mind to manipulate her. *The daughter of the Rebels, I’m going to have fun,* he thought then. Not only had she already figured him out—thanks to her own gifts—and blocked her mind, but she had also punched him in the stomach. A most tumultuous friendship had begun.

“He is going to be so easy to manipulate,” Jesse tells the others telepathically.

“What happens on the other side?” Jesse asks the Commander, pointing to the uncontrolled areas of the town.

Tabitha is giddy with pleasure. She loves to see Jesse start controlling another mind. It's so amoral. It's almost impossible to resist him. Jesse concentrates and the Commander does not understand why he begins to tell the story while continuing to walk towards the limits of "his" city.

"All these years, I've seen them coming from Kantas City, and more and more of them. They crammed in here. Some of them are leaving. Others stay. Gradually, we lost control of the city. We continued to have interventions and even extra-judicial executions, but we were no longer intimidating anyone. So now we provide food, clothing, basic goods, and so we keep the peace."

They are standing in front of a large wrought iron door. Jesse concentrates and feels that the Commander's brain is hiding important information from him. Finally, he manages to break through.

"To keep control, I introduced one of my teams inside. They have instigated a real gang war. Their leader is called Cronos."

The Commander remains silent for a few minutes. Jesse releases him from his mental control. The Commander then slowly looks at each of them.

"But who are you?" he asks in a fearful tone.

"Commander, we're going to spend a bit of time there. This discussion will remain between us, as well as what we will do there. Otherwise...."

Jesse trails off, giving him a glacial stare.

"Otherwise, you're going to have to deal with us."

The Commander shivers despite the heat. Now he wonders if there really is any danger for them beyond this door, or if those who live there are the ones in danger.

The four advance down the alleys, all senses heightened and their weapons unlimbered and ready for use. Tabitha, with her exceptional hearing, gives them a direct account of the number of occupants in the buildings around them.

Whenever she wishes, Tabitha can hear everything that is said for kilometers around. She often uses this gift as a formidable weapon. "Having information is strategic, Tabitha," her mother told her. Despite their often-difficult relationships, Ariane has never told anyone about her daughter's gift.

As the Commander has told them, the neighborhood is completely overcrowded and yet there is no one on the streets. The people are apparently hiding in buildings and makeshift barracks. The arrival of their shuttle did not go unnoticed. A vehicle of this caliber can only belong to the Government. Tabitha hears the fear, the cries of the children, the shivers as they pass by.

"The situation is explosive," Tabitha whispers.

Cathy and Jesse walk in front, looking for signs of armed men. Tabitha and then James follow them. James remains mainly behind, looking for signs of danger. Thanks to his great stature, he is a shield to protect his friends. Finally, after a few minutes of high tension in a dilapidated street, they reach a completely empty square. On all sides of the square there are deserted and messy stands, signs of a sudden departure. The square is large and seems to be the main place of activity of the city. Hundreds of people must surely be crowded together at any time. But when the four friends enter, they feel isolated and particularly exposed. Cathy and Jesse continue to walk towards the center.

"Guys, I would feel better if we were near an exit," James tells them.

"We've already thrown ourselves into the lion's den," Jesse replies.

"They are coming," says Tabitha.

The four friends are now in the center of the square, back to back, their weapons in position, ready to fire if necessary. People are finally showing up. A real crowd, hundreds of men and women armed with knives, sticks and even a few guns.

"Wow, that's very impressive," says Cathy.

But her voice is not nervous. It is full of excitement.

"You're crazy, Cathy," Tabitha replies. "You do realize where we are right now? Surrounded by Rebels! Our enemies!"

The people before them are all about fifteen to thirty years old. Their clothes are mismatched and show extreme poverty. Yet their demeanor shows excellent physical condition and signs of combat training.

"That's amazing. How is it possible that we never knew there were so many of them here, and so close to Kantas City? It's incredible," says James.

"Frankly, I can't imagine that my father doesn't know," Jesse says. "They simply made us live in a bubble, literally and figuratively!"

The crowd is now about ten meters away and forming a circle around them.

Suddenly, one of them breaks away. He walks forward with purposeful nonchalance.

"Wow! What a hottie," whispers Cathy to Tabitha.

"Stop being an idiot," Tabitha replies.

The hottie in question smiles at them from the corner of his mouth.

"He's definitely resourceful," says Cathy, who has noticed that he can also read their lips.

"Hello Cathy, Tabitha, Jesse, and James. Welcome to Toledo. We are all delighted to have you here," he says, pointing to the crowd whose faces suggest otherwise.

The four friends look at him and listen carefully. He looks only a few years older than they, but he has such confidence in his voice and his movement that there is no doubt that he is the leader of the crowd. He's tall, blond with brown eyes. His has full lips, which contrast with his Roman nose. But what makes him particularly attractive is the defiance in his gaze, highlighted by golden, tan skin.

"They call me Poseidon."

The four look at each other with astonishment

"Zeus told me you were coming," he adds. "Here, among us, you are safe."

"How do you communicate with him? How did he know we were leaving Kantas City?" Cathy asks eagerly.

"Everything in its own time. I have some questions too. You started your journey in Toledo. Was it just because it was near Kantas City or is there a specific reason?"

Poseidon, who must have felt the hesitation of the young Elites, adds:

"You've trusted Zeus so far, you can continue with me."

"No! Chris trusts Zeus, but I don't," says Tabitha.

She raises her weapon. Jesse and James do the same.

Cathy makes a gesture of appeasement in their direction and says:

“My mother’s great friend came here years ago when I was a very young girl. They were like sisters and I would like to find her again.”

“Do you have her registration number?”

“I just have her Rebel name.”

Cathy stops. Saying her name is like opening an old wound.

“I know she was called Beatrix.”

When this name is mentioned, Poseidon freezes. He watches Cathy intensely for a few seconds that feel like hours.

“Beatrix is here,” he says.

He pauses.

“She’s probably living her last few days. I don’t know if you can talk to her.”

Cathy shudders at these words.

“I have to see her,” she begs. “I may never get the answers to my questions if I don’t see her.”

James, Tabitha, and Jesse look at each other, surprised to see Cathy so upset.

“I can go get Leah if you want,” says James, touched by his friend’s distress.

“Shall I come with you?” asks Tabitha.

“Stay here with the others. I can manage on my own,”

Tabitha scowls in frustration.

“He can go with a dozen of my companions, for more safety, at least to the door,” suggests Poseidon. “The streets are not so safe these days.”

On that note, he waves to some of the men and women behind him, who then start running towards the door. James goes after them.

"Go on James. Go join your escort, mademoiselle," teases Jesse.

Tabitha laughs, more out of nervousness than humor.

"We're going to see Beatrix," continues Poseidon, focused on his objective. He turns around, gives orders to everyone, some to follow him, others to resume their activities.

"What do you think of him, Cathy?" Jesse asks telepathically. *"I've been trying but I can't get into his mind. He pisses me off."*

"He does indeed have a strong mind. He also gives me a lot of trouble. What I do feel, however, is that he has a very strong sense of justice. I have a feeling we can trust him. It's just a feeling. Or maybe that's what I'd like. I don't know. It's weird."

"I find him very arrogant," Tabitha tells them.

Jesse and Cathy look at each other with smiles on their faces.

Poseidon approaches them, interrupting their unheard conversation.

"Let's go, it's this way. But be careful from here on."

Poseidon naturally takes the lead of the group and heads for an adjacent alley. The inhabitants start to come out and the square fills up in a flash. A human barrier forms around them as they move forward. Cathy can't help but enjoy the moment. Here it's like Obama, but much more alive. The crowd is heterogeneous, different ages, different skin colors, and mismatched clothes. The crowd studies them with curiosity. The Elite uniforms are so beautiful in contrast to theirs. Of course, they watch the pretty green-eyed blonde, Cathy, the legend, the young Elite whose mother lives in Obama. But above all, they look at the "Prince" and the "Princess."

Jesse enjoys feeling the excitement rushing through his body, walking through a Rebel neighborhood. Never before have they broken the rules so much. Because it is clear to them now that this is indeed a city populated almost entirely by Rebels.

Tabitha, unlike the others, walks with less confidence than usual. *They could kill us in a heartbeat—we, the future leaders of the Red World. What kind of mess did Cathy get us into?* she wonders.

Poseidon posts some companions in front of them and others behind them. He appears to be focused on the road and occasionally gives instructions or waves to companions lining the way. At least ten minutes pass before they reach a house a little beyond the alley. Heavily armed men and women sit in front and quickly stand up when the procession arrives. Poseidon exchanges fraternal hugs with some of them and waves to Cathy, Jesse, and Tabitha to come forward.

"This is our Elite of Toledo," he says, pointing to his companions.

The physical condition and reflexes they demonstrate impress the young Elites. *And if Poseidon left them in front of this house,* they say to themselves, *it's because there's something or someone important inside.*

"This is Beatrix's house," says Poseidon. "Let's go in and see her."

They walk through rooms occupied with files and computers, where several people work.

"Chris would be going crazy here," Jesse says laughing.

Finally, they come to a room where a blonde woman, who appears to be around fifty years old, is lying on an old mattress. Several people are watching over her.

"Beatrix, you have visitors," Poseidon whispers to her quietly. She slowly turns her head in what appears to be a superhuman effort. She looks at the arrivals with astonishment, but when she looks at Cathy, a big smile lights up her face.

"Cathy, is it really you?" she asks in a weak voice.

Cathy walks in with tears in her eyes. She was hoping so much that this woman would be there. Seeing her emaciated face, her olive skin, her ash-blonde hair streaked with white, causes a strong surge of emotion and buried memories to come to the surface.

"Where is your mother?" asks Beatrix, searching around her.

"She's not with me. She stayed in Obama," Cathy says in her softest voice.

"That's odd, I saw her yesterday."

Cathy looks at Poseidon, who nods to Beatrix to continue.

"And yet she didn't want to come with me and run away—all because of you. She wanted you to become an Elite. You had the Mark. This damn Mark." Beatrix stops and looks at Cathy. "You look beautiful in your Elite uniform. But you grew up fast."

She turns to face Poseidon as if nothing had happened.

"My son, I'm a little tired now. Can you ask your friends to leave the room?"

"Are you her son?" Jesse asks.

"Let's leave her and talk outside," Poseidon says.

They quickly withdraw from the room. Beatrix is lying on her side and she has already closed her eyes.

"Now I remember you, Cathy," says Poseidon at last. "I never made the connection."

"Are you kidding me? You're Beatrix's son," Cathy replies angrily.

"Oh, my God, calm down, both of you," Jesse tells them.

"Yes, now Cathy, you owe us an explanation," Tabitha continues, arms crossed. "I want to understand too."

Cathy takes a deep breath and looks to Jesse trying to find an ally in her. He also looks at her with a quizzical expression.

"Okay," Cathy says. "Beatrix was my mother's best friend. I remember as a child that they were always together. Then my mother and father were arrested by the Government. She ran away." Cathy stops and looks at Poseidon. "She ran away with her son."

She pauses.

"My mother was saying you were an extraordinary child. They had to hide you."

"Hide me? What does that mean?" asks Poseidon.

"I don't know about that. When she came home, after weeks of torture, she was completely different. But at night, when I was a little girl, I often heard her saying, 'Go away, Beatrix. Go away and take your son.'"

The memory of her mother makes Cathy feel sick.

"What else do you know?" asks Poseidon with urgency.

Cathy shakes her head.

"Anything else? Are you sure you're not hiding anything else?" Tabitha insists angrily.

"No, I swear," pleads Cathy. "How am I supposed to know anything else? My mother is barely able to take care of herself. She doesn't talk to me about anything. I had completely forgotten about Beatrix and her son. It came back to me when we left and talked about going to Toledo. Now I want to understand too."

"And you, Poseidon?" asks Jesse.

"There's nothing for me to tell either. As you saw, my mother has completely lost her mind. And I didn't even know that Cathy, Cathy the Elite, was the little girl I saw from time to time with my mother."

"You're kidding us," Jesse replies. "You're strutting like a peacock with your army of losers, but you don't know anything either!"

Poseidon looks at him very calmly.

"Oh yes, I know something now. You're really an asshole like everyone says."

Jesse laughs.

"I knew I would like you."

The two men look at each other with smiles on their faces. Tabitha and Cathy roll their eyes.

"Wow, what a macho game!" exclaims Tabitha.

James and Leah come into the room at that moment.

"Are we interrupting an important discussion or something?" asks James.

Leah, not waiting for the answer, asks eagerly:

"So, where is this Beatrix?"

"This way," Poseidon says, taking her with him into the room they had all just left.

Leah sits next to Beatrix and gently touches her forehead. She closes her eyes and moves her hands in circular movements over Beatrix's body as she sleeps. A wild energy is released making Leah's pretty red curls twirl. Her round face, dotted with freckles, looks so child-like. Yet she is powerful. She begins to murmur an incantation and a light now surrounds them both.

The crowd keeps very still while watching the ritual for a few minutes. Leah explains.

"She has a kind of senile dementia; that is, she no longer knows where she is and what day it is. Her short-term memory no longer exists. She can't remember what she said or what she saw a few minutes before, can she?"

Several people nod their heads in agreement.

"There is nothing I can do to help her, unfortunately," says Leah in a soft voice. "However, her general condition could improve if she ate certain foods with the vitamins she lacks."

She grabs a paper lying near her and starts scribbling a list of products.

"This may be difficult to find, but frankly, any one of the five will do."

She is now looking at Poseidon and Cathy.

"It's not natural. She was poisoned."

Poseidon doesn't seem surprised to hear it. Violence is part of his daily life, and despite his precautions, Beatrix has always been the target of Red Army attacks.

One of Poseidon's companions bursts into the room with a loud crash.

"There's an attack outside, come quickly!"

Poseidon, the five Elites, and the armed companions rush out, running through the corridors to reach the entrance of the house as quickly as possible.

Outside about twenty men and women are fighting on each side. The attackers are easily recognizable because they all wear black clothes and black balaclavas. The Elites quickly notice that some seem to have come straight out of the Red Army training camps.

"Come on, guys, I'd like to have a go at those bozos," Jesse says with excitement.

"It's really not your fight," Poseidon replies.

"I know, but just for fun, please," begs Jesse with a smile.

"It really is not your fight and frankly, I don't think your father would appreciate it if you beat up soldiers who attack Rebels," says Tabitha.

A glimmer of mischief runs through her eyes.

"Go have fun, go! But don't hurt them too much," she adds.

Poseidon cannot hide his astonishment. Leah approaches him and puts one hand on his shoulder.

"Don't worry, we're not all like him. He likes to fight a lot."

What follows is a surreal scene where Poseidon, his companions, and the four remaining Elites look at Jesse proudly, with his beautiful Elite uniform, joining the fight. With disconcerting ease and a mixture of ancient martial arts techniques, he takes the attackers down, one after the other. Poseidon's companions stop fighting and watch Jesse. The attackers are now all around him, but at the sight of his terrifying superiority, they finally decide to beat a hasty retreat.

"Hey, come back! We were just starting to have fun!"

Poseidon's companions look at Jesse with dismay, but also with great respect.

"You didn't even see James in full action!" Leah tells Poseidon.

"But what are you?" Poseidon asks them.

"Very good question," Cathy answers with a dark look. "Weapons, monsters, kids looking for answers."

"When you do find out, I hope we're on the same side." He looks at them with a mocking smile.

"You're going away for ten days, right?" he adds. "On the last day, the ninth day, stop here and I'll organize an evening for you. Then you'll see what it's really like to party. I'm sure you're all a little cramped in your Elite Center."

"You haven't met Max yet," replies Leah. "You'll be surprised."

"No. I'm the coolest guy in the world," Jesse can't help but add.

They all look at each other smiling. A silent pact is made.

As the Elites return to the entrance of the city, Poseidon grabs Tabitha by the arm and says to her, "I can see you don't trust me."

And he adds, but this time in a murmur, "When you come back, I hope you'll agree to dance with me."

Tabitha turns around coolly but inside she can feel herself steaming.

"He really has some nerve!"

SOMEWHERE UNDERGROUND, 2027, ADRIEN

------------ *Adrien, "underground", 2027*
------------ *Indigo, Paris, 2025*
------------ *Sarah, United States, 2022*

EVERY NIGHT, I WAKE up. It is dark around me. My cohabitants don't make noise anymore and I can start dreaming about my mountains. It has been two years since those who have the Mark were locked in their underground nuclear bunkers. "That's great, we were chosen. We are the chosen ones! You must remain confident, Adrien," my lifelong friend, Indigo, tells me again when she sees my discouragement, despite the fortress I am trying to build around my feelings. Some people crack and ask to go back up. God only knows what happens to them after that. I, myself, don't know what to think. I'm a mountain dweller, for God's sake, not an underground rat! The person in charge of our block regularly gives us news from above. Just a few months more and we can come back up.

So, I start dreaming about my mountains—Luchon, my queen of the Pyrenees, surrounded by her majestic mountains. I see myself going up the Larboust Valley. Only a few more kilometers and I will see my village of Trébons. My village is very small, but it has been perfectly placed on the mountain, in a spot where it is always sunny. During my regular escapades in Larboust, I see it, my little village, proud and bathed in sunshine. In the foreground, I can see the church, just like a scene out of a postcard. A church so small that it was never possible for everyone to squeeze inside for services. But that's where my father is buried, and that's where I'll rest too—I, a Cazala de Trébons. It is such a small village that only about a dozen people live there—or lived there, I should say. Before these damned Ecological Wars broke out and more than 99.99% of the population was exterminated.

I often wonder what it must be like to live above ground and how many of us are left.

Indigo, my journalist friend, always aware of everything that is going on—curse of the profession, she tells me—says that the Gulf Stream has gone out of control, parts of Europe and the United States are underwater, that the explosions of all nuclear power plants have eradicated most of the fauna and flora.

I cannot imagine that my mountains and my village are any more. So, I keep dreaming, to make sure they continue to exist. I see my house, 300 years old, located in the center of the village. The former school and town hall of the village, which has seen several generations of Cazala, live, eat, laugh, love, cry. I see the chimney that is big enough to keep all the siblings cozy and warm on cold winter evenings. It was in this room that in the spring, with my brother Estéban and my little sister Pauline, we decided which paths we would take to go and explore. There, where in summer, we would take refuge in the coolness of the thick walls. There, where in the fall, we deposited our treasures: hand-picked mushrooms that my mother and sisters would prepare.

The sound of the general alarm pulls me out of my dreams.

A few more months. I will succeed because I, Adrien Cazala de Trébons, am a strong man. I am a man from the mountains.

CHAPTER 12

DEPARTURE FROM TOLEDO AND RETURN TO THE STATION

Day 2 of the trip continued, year 2125

ON THEIR RETURN FROM their escapade in Toledo, Chris, Stephanie, and Max bombard their friends with questions, to which Leah and Jesse enthusiastically answer. They are still in shock at having had to deal with so many Rebels in a city so close to Kantas City. They describe in great detail everything they saw, what was said and what they did.

Tabitha and Cathy have locked themselves in a deep silence.

As soon as he enters the shuttle, James sits in the cockpit and prepares to leave. First of all, he doesn't especially like to talk, but more importantly, he doesn't yet know what to think about what has happened in the last few hours. Tabitha settles next to him. Without a word, Tabitha and James start their shuttle and leave Toledo.

They settle quite far from the city, sheltered by a rocky ledge.

"While you were in Toledo, Chris, Stephanie and I organized a party for you," Max exclaimed.

"I read that before the Ecological Wars, young people loved camping, singing and dancing around a campfire," adds Stephanie.

"I've filled up on music that we'd like you to discover," Chris continues. "You'll see: rock and rap are so cool!"

As soon as the heat falls, the young people settle outside and prepare a fire. They find it a little strange at first, but Max's good mood, helped by his guitar, quickly relaxes everyone. A battle of improvisation and invented songs follows.

In Kantas City, only a soothing and relaxing sound is allowed. Yet that doesn't stop some young people from finding a way to make music. That there are so many instruments in the shuttle remains a mystery to them.

"That's because I'm the favorite of the group," Max suggests. "They wanted to please me."

"Yet Stephanie and I should be the favorites. We are the smartest," Chris replies.

"No, it's me, because I'm the most handsome, of course," Jesse says.

Then James shows his developed muscles and compares himself to Jesse, causing everyone to laugh.

They marvel at the colors that fall on the ground. On their horizon, a shade of crimson to pale yellow blends with the blue of the sky, producing a light green layer. The heat on the rocks disperses a sweet smell with a hint of burned caramel. They realize how much they've been trapped living in the Dome, isolated from the beauty of the planet, its colors and smells.

"If the Leaders left Kantas City just like we have, how could they return to their lives in Black and White?" asks Max.

"Life in Black and White is a very beautiful image. That's exactly what it is," James adds.

"For all we know, not everything will be as beautiful as this sunset. It's obvious that they had to go through things that made them prefer to go on with their lives as if nothing had happened," adds Stephanie.

"Like nothing happened? You're joking, Stephanie," exclaims Cathy. "The current Government has been much more authoritarian than the previous ones. Ask Obama's people, those who have lost family."

"And there it is. Cathy shows her true face," says Tabitha with a dismissive look. "Our little Rebel is creating a crisis."

"Oh you, the Princess, the privileged one, the one who has no idea what it is like to suffer because of the Government," says Cathy, standing up now, ready to fight her.

"Girls, calm down," Max says. "What's the matter with you?"

"She started attacking me first in Toledo," replies Cathy sulking.

"Do you see yourself? Just out of Kantas City and you openly show your sympathy for the Rebels," Tabitha says, again on the offensive.

"That's rubbish," Cathy interrupts her. "I just wanted to find out about my mother's friend, that's all."

It feels very cold around Cathy and Tabitha.

"My family, my priority, is you and it will always be you," Cathy tells them, in an intense voice. "Never doubt it."

"Okay, okay, so now it's our night out. It's over. We're going to rest," Leah says in an authoritative voice.

She's pretending to return to the shuttle.

"Girls, don't worry, it'll be all right," Chris tells them.

"Stop with the 'don't worry,'" Cathy and Tabitha say in chorus.

Everyone starts laughing in front of Chris' fallen face.

They go to bed, their heads full of new feelings, but with their hearts heavy after the altercation between Cathy and Tabitha.

Day 3 of the trip, year 2125

"Of course, I really want to spend this evening in Toledo on the ninth day, but we're still going to Canfranc station this morning, aren't we?" asks Leah.

"That's the tenth time you've asked since you woke up. Yes, we're going," Stephanie replies.

"Don't worry, Leah," Chris says. "James checked the flight plan. We will have time to go to Canfranc, to inspect what is happening around the two geographical coordinates and to return to Toledo on the ninth day."

"All right, let's go! Hold on tight! "James says to them.

They now marvel at the beauty of the mountains around them. A thick mantle of snow covers all the peaks. Steep valleys appear here and there, giving the possibility of passageways that could mean the presence of humans. They are moving slowly in search of makeshift housing.

"Do you really think people can survive on this terrain?" Tabitha wonders aloud to James, who sits next to her in the cockpit.

"These places were populated before, but it was certainly not as cold then. It's beautiful, don't you think? There is something soothing about looking at these steep peaks."

"Mm," she replies, absorbed by her screen. "I think we're on our way. Leah! Leah! Come on, Leah, does that mean anything to you?" Tabitha asks, pointing at the screen.

Leah approaches the cockpit. The others follow her immediately.

"Yes, absolutely. Oh, look!"

A valley opens up in front of them. And at the bottom, the old railway station appears, a hundred meters long, with its dozens of rails starting on each side and entering four separate tunnels.

The shuttle lands gently on the snow cover.

All eight of them exit, not detecting any presence nearby, all curious to discover—or rediscover for some—this 20th-century building.

They have armed themselves and are slowly advancing toward, then into, the building, their senses alert. Some of them look in the adjoining rooms, or what's left of them. Their torches are reflected on the broken windows and on the ceiling where frescoes from another time stand out.

"What do you think, Max?" asks Stephanie. "These look like early 20th-century fresco details."

"Yes, even if they seem to be repeating scenes from the Bible," he replies. "It looks like the Last Supper, with Jesus and his Twelve Apostles. We must be in what must have been a fairly religious area."

"Maybe it was originally a church. Look at the vaults," Stephanie says to him.

Max and Stephanie have stopped walking, and are staring in awe at the display around them. "The techniques are undoubtedly 20th century, what they called modern architecture," adds Stephanie.

"It's magnificent," exclaims Max. "Why doesn't the Red World preserve these wonders? What beauty!"

Suddenly, noises can be heard a little further into the building.

"Don't shoot," Max tells them. "They are just animals. I'll take care of it."

At that moment, several animals come out and look in their direction, growling disconcertingly. Max responds with a similar sound. They are a cross-breed of dog and wolf, certainly the result of natural selection to be able to survive in these areas after the events of 2025.

Max grunts several more times. His mouth is distorted. Even his body seems to change at the sight of the animals.

What an extraordinary gift, thinks Cathy, reflecting that she would have preferred to understand animals instead of humans.

Max explains, "They just arrived because the people have gone and they thought they were going to find food. In fact, they have found some, but they are willing to leave it for us for a few minutes."

"Leave what?" asks Leah, worried.

"The bodies that are near them."

"Oh no, that's not possible," she says with a sigh.

"The animals will slowly retreat while we examine the bodies," says Max. "Frankly, they are very numerous and very dangerous, and we should do what they suggest."

"Okay, let's go fast. I don't really want to fight an army of thirsty wolf-dogs," James adds.

The animals slowly retreat while showing their teeth and bright, red eyes. Behind them, there is the body of a young woman holding in her arms a little girl who is not quite ten years old.

Leah runs to kneel next to them. She touches the little girl. Her body is still warm. A moan escapes from Leah's mouth.

"What's the matter?" James asks, worried.

"We should have come earlier. I feel bad about it. Why did I listen to you? They probably stayed behind the others in order to wait for us," she says in a voice close to hysteria.

"Leah," interrupts Stephanie. "Take a deep breath and answer my questions. First, what did they die of? And second, could you have saved them?"

Leah exhales gently, closes her eyes, and touches the little girl's forehead for a few seconds.

"The girl, type 1 diabetes. I couldn't have saved her." Leah sighs, before adding: "If only she had been brought back to Kantas City, she would have been cured in a few days."

"One advantage of Kantas City is that it has such advanced health care," says Tabitha.

"A point for you, Tabitha," Cathy adds.

"And the young woman?" asks James.

"It must be her mother, given her physical resemblance," says Leah. "She must have let herself die near her daughter. Look at how she's holding her."

This elicits a palpable emotion. No one dares to speak until Tabitha breaks the silence.

"Well, my mother would not do that for me."

"Nor mine, if anyone's asking," James says in a whisper.

Grunts are heard a short distance away.

"Well, now, I think we're going to have to go," says Jesse. "Our carnivorous friends are getting impatient."

"It's horrible, we can't let that happen," says Stephanie.

"They're already dead, so let them eat," Jesse says.

"Unless, Stephanie, you want to face a pack of rabid animals," Max adds. "What are our chances, James?"

"Of course, I can fight these animals. But why kill them, the poor creatures?"

Leah looks at them with tears in her eyes, quickly pulls out her dagger and cuts off a finger from the young woman and then from the young girl.

"Run!" she shouts.

The wild animals have smelled the odor of blood and are rushing in their direction. However, they stop near the bodies, obviously judging that there is still enough food left for them.

The Eight don't turn around until they're in the shuttle.

"What was the big idea, Leah? Are you trying to get us killed or what?" Jesse asks, surprised and out of breath.

"It's something Cathy said the other day. She says they were pure. I want to check something."

With Chris' help, Leah pulls out her equipment, microscope, and computer, while James and Tabitha are already at their posts, ready to go.

"Should we go now?" asks James.

"Let's go around the area first," Cathy replies. "You never know, we might find their tracks."

"I still can't understand who these people are, where they came from, how they can survive in such conditions," Stephanie continues.

"They don't all survive, as you can see," Leah says in a dry tone.

"They must be in one of the tunnels," Jesse says, pointing at them. "Which would explain why we don't have a signal."

"It's going to be a lot harder to find them," says Cathy.

"Who wants a little trip in a tunnel with hungry hell-hounds?" asks Jesse to no one in particular.

"Put me underground? No thanks," James replies. "Isn't there a river somewhere? Even if it's frozen, I'll take it."

"I'll leave the survivors to you," adds Tabitha, who is already starting the engines.

"Whoa, what the hell?" exclaims Chris, his eyes glued to his screen.

Leah is next to him, feverishly handling the DNA samples. The others turn to them.

"Whoa, this is absolutely crazy!" he continues.

"So, please tell us, Chris," asks Jesse.

"Your people at the train station—well, the two girls who are now being eaten there—they are not from our race. We are not of the same race!"

SOMEWHERE IN THE PÉRIGORD IN FRANCE, 2006, ANNA

------------ *Adrien, "underground", 2027*
------------ *Indigo, Paris, 2025*
------------ *Sarah, United States, 2022*
------------ *Anna, Lascaux, France, 2006*

HER SISTER, AN ANTHROPOLOGIST at the University of California in Los Angeles, had left with some colleagues to do research near the Lascaux caves. There were still so many unexplored caves in the area. The prospect of a discovery combined with good French wine and magnificent landscapes convinced them to spend a few months in the area.

They spoke once a week, always on Sundays, so she was surprised to receive an SMS telling her: "Come and join me. Now! It's urgent. Take the first plane, please, and don't forget your gear."

That's why they're both now squatting at the bottom of a tiny little cave, several meters underground, searching with their infrared lights.

"Are you sure the others don't know about this?"

"I'm telling you, they've gone to Paris for a few days. I wanted to be alone for a while, and as soon as they left, I came across it."

"It's still so beautiful. Look at the drawings of horses and bulls. Beautiful! Beautiful!"

"A beautiful grave for our friend, that's for sure."

"How old do you think he is?"

"Seventeen or eighteen thousand years old. And I have a feeling you're going to find something interesting."

"Of course, it's going to be interesting. Look at the Mark!"

And the two sisters can admire the pattern reproduced dozens of time across the ceiling, a pattern that they also have on their left shoulders.

Later, after she had returned to San Francisco, she sends this message to her sister: "You have to close the cave permanently. Your suspicion was right. I will create a company that will offer its customers the analysis of their genetic code. It will take years, but we'll find them."

CHAPTER 13

THE LONG JOURNEY

Day 3 of the trip continued, year 2125

JAMES AND TABITHA FLY the shuttle around the station and the surrounding mountains, looking for survivors. They manage to land in other valleys but find no trace of human activity. After several hours of scouting, the impatience spreads through the group.

"Have they evaporated, or what?" Jesse asks.

"They hide in tunnels," Cathy says. "Either we go for a hike underground that may take us several days and maybe get us lost, or we drop it."

"We drop it," Tabitha lashes out.

"I agree with my girlfriends," Jesse adds.

"Can you imagine? They're not from our race! It's an extraordinary thing," exclaims Chris.

"Yes, but we have a plan to follow," Cathy reminds them. "We decided to join the two geographical coordinates and then return to Toledo on the ninth day."

"Stephanie, help me," begs Chris.

'I'm sorry, Chris. If my information is correct, we have to go to the other side of the world, somewhere in former Oceania, and it's going to be a very long journey," her friend tells her.

"Almost two days," James adds.

"They're right, Chris," says Leah. "It breaks my heart, but we're wasting our time here."

"Okay, let's leave these beautiful mountains," concludes James.

With an expert hand, he changes direction and heads south.

They travel hundreds of kilometers, still in the Red World. They stay away from cities.

"That's it, we're leaving home," Tabitha tells them. "Now we don't have any more information about what we're going to see."

"Do you know why the Government wants to keep the geography of the world so secret before and after the Ecological Wars of 2025?" asks James.

Before Tabitha can answer, Jesse says, "Because if it's so much better elsewhere. Everyone would leave Kantas City."

"That's right," says Tabitha laughing. "Obviously it is not to explore, conquer, and destroy the world a second time," she adds seriously.

"Do you think that's the real reason?" asks James, doubtful.

"We're about to find out," Jesse says. "What do you know about our destination, 'walking dictionary?'"

"Thank you, Jesse," replies Stephanie, slapping him on the back. "I think we're going to an island, New Zealand."

"What?! That's not where they all played rugby, is it?" asks Max, who is following the conversation from afar.

"It's an island, and they play my favorite sport, it's going to be great," exclaims James.

"You think when we get there they'll be waiting for us on the playing field and they'll say, 'Come on, guys, let's have a little game?'" Jesse says to him.

"There may not be anything at all," offers Tabitha.

"Zeus wouldn't send us to the other side of the world for nothing," Chris says.

"Who knows, maybe he is trying to get rid of us," Tabitha replies.

"That's impossible. There will be something important there, I'm sure of it," says Chris. His left leg begins to shake nervously, and he holds on to keep from falling.

"Oh, my friend, calm down," James says, putting his strong hands around his shoulders.

"Yes, Chris, don't worry," Jesse mimics.

This makes everyone laugh, even Chris himself.

Leah and Cathy are following the conversation from a distance. They look out over the desert plains that stretch around as far as the eye can see.

"You look worried, Leah."

"Maybe I still haven't recovered from the shock of our discoveries in Canfranc."

"There is an explanation. Perhaps there have always been several races of man. What do we know about it anyway? I have the feeling that we are only at the beginning of our discoveries."

"Thank you, Cathy, for always being there for me."

"Of course, you're my favorite! Come on, let's take over from James and Tabitha, so they can rest."

Day 4 of the trip, year 2125

They travel all night taking breaks in turns. Their shuttle uses rechargeable solar-powered batteries. They have enough energy to last them several days.

Almost everywhere, they can see only deserts, intact forests, and mountains. How could the Earth, which used to shelter billions of human beings, have eliminated all trace of their existence? From time to time they see groups of animals, always in hordes and in vast numbers. The young Elites, by instinct, try not to get too close to them, as animals never get closer than hundreds of kilometers from the Dome. Stephanie declares that it is because humans have enslaved them; some of them have even been completely exterminated. Since then, those who have survived nuclear disasters have evolved and learned to be wary. Stephanie and Max beg their friends to fly nearby. Max is eager to communicate with them. But Tabitha is reluctant to approach.

"Don't worry, Tabitha, my dear. I'll always be by your side to protect you," Max says teasingly.

"But how do you know that they will *all* be able to understand you? And more to the point, that they'll do what you ask them to do?"

"I just know that that's the way it is. However, following my instructions is another matter. Besides, I wasn't much of a confident dude yesterday with the wolf-dogs. I was quite scared!"

"You're completely crazy."

"Welcome to the Club. We're all completely crazy, my dear."

Tabitha nods in agreement. After all, who else in the world can hear like her, or communicate with animals like Max? Tabitha tells herself that it's because they're superior to others, but now and then a little voice in her head suggests to her that it's because something is not right with them.

They are now crossing a large body of water and it's James' turn to act crazy.

"Will you look at that, guys? It's incredible! Hold me back or I'll just dive off the shuttle now."

"New Zealand is an island. If that's where we're going, you'll have plenty of time to enjoy it," answers Cathy, who could also be tempted by a little bath.

Chris and Stephanie continue to type on computers looking for information and maps that could give them directions, because the prospect of staying hours over the ocean doesn't appeal to them.

"We've only known the shuttle for three days and we can't rule out a mechanical failure," Chris tells them.

"Yes, I think we have to go back north," says Stephanie.

Tabitha changes the direction of the shuttle. After a few minutes, they are flying over desert plains. Everything looks almost white as if a layer of snow has covered the surface. But with those ambient temperatures, it cannot be snow.

"Look outside, everyone. It is absolutely incredible. There's nothing," James tells his friends.

"We have to check the levels of radioactivity," says Stephanie decidedly.

Everyone turns to her.

"Come on, let's go down," Jesse adds.

The shuttle slowly descends to the surface of the Earth, and now they can see that what they thought was snow is actually a kind of foamy mass, with small craters in places from which brownish lava flows.

"We're not going to land here, that's for sure," Jesse adds. "But can we still calculate the level of radioactivity?"

"Yes, we have sensors around the shuttle," Chris replies. "Just give me a few seconds."

Stephanie, who is hovering above him, cannot hold back a cry of surprise.

"Oh no! We are at levels at least 300 times higher than around the Dome."

"The wars must have been terrible here," Jesse says.

"Indeed," replies Stephanie. "What happened here must have been so terrible that a hundred years later the Earth cannot regenerate itself."

"I overheard a conversation from my mother saying that the wars started at the cradle of Western civilization," says Tabitha.

"Well, we're right on the mark," Jesse adds.

"Guys, I don't think we should hang around here," says James, who is already bringing the shuttle up to a more comfortable altitude.

"How could mankind kill each other and ruin everything?" asks Leah.

"Religious wars, the quest for power," replies Stephanie.

"Greed, selfishness, intolerance, stupidity," adds Cathy. "And I can give you even more reasons. Our species did not deserve this planet, that's for sure."

"Now girls, don't get depressed," Max says. "There are still some nice humans. Look at me!"

Max starts making faces, while improvising uncertain dance steps, causing everyone to laugh and relaxing the atmosphere.

SOMEWHERE IN THE MIDDLE EAST, 2025, FADI

------------ *Adrien, "underground", 2027*
------------ *Indigo, Paris, 2025*
------------ *Fadi, Egypt, 2025*
------------ *Sarah, United States, 2022*
------------ *Anna, Lascaux, France, 2006*

THE GODS HAVE NOT forgiven us. How could they do that? Just yesterday, a fifteen-year-old girl entered a daycare in Jerusalem and blew herself up. The carnage was such that it was impossible to distinguish each of the thirty small corpses, aged four and five. "It is Jewish extremists' fault," some shouted. "It's the Muslim terrorists' fault," called others. "It's America's fault. They have fueled the flames between the different communities," we could hear. "It's the Europeans' fault, the

Russians' fault, China's fault, the United Nations Security Council's fault."

I believe that it is simply man's fault. Man, who has not understood the words of love and tolerance of the different gods, prophets, messiahs and other emissaries.

I am sitting in this beautiful creek, by the water, and the fine, clear sand trickles between my fingers. Behind me are the ruins of the red ochre buildings, an old tourist hotel that was abandoned decades ago. The area is far too dangerous. Opposite, I can see the coast of Saudi Arabia, then on the left, the Jordanian coast. Continuing in my direction, at the end of the Gulf, is the Israeli coast, and I am sitting in Egyptian territory—all this in the space of a few kilometers. Everywhere there are rock formations ranging in color from beige to ochre, some even tinted with purple.

It is so beautiful.

I have fought all these years for justice to return to this world, for the oppressed to be protected, for the righteous to be recognized and celebrated.

I'm coming to the end of my journey.

Only one more day.

I am ready.

CHAPTER 14

IN THE JUNGLE

Day 5 of the trip, year 2125

AFTER HAVING CROSSED THE apocalyptic zone, as Jesse calls it, the day before, they then passed desert landscapes to finally reach majestic and higher mountains at dawn. Unfortunately, the weather is turning bad and they have to climb as high as they can to avoid turbulence, making it impossible to explore this area. They then cross vast expanses of forest to finally reach the sea in the early morning.

For a few hours now they have been flying over islands that seemed uninhabited and particularly inhospitable, with impenetrable forests. When they descend to less than a hundred meters above the islands, Max sometimes perceives very intense animal activity. The absence of humans has allowed animal species to adapt in surprising ways to their new environment.

James and Jesse are now in control, flying over a small island, under pressure from Max, who is continuing his studies on animal behavior.

"There, down there!" exclaims Tabitha, who was dozing off in a corner of her cabin.

She rushes to the cockpit and pushes Jesse hard.

"There, underneath. I hear noises!" she says.

"So do I," adds Cathy, who joins them. "I sense a human presence. Quick, let's check it out."

"And there are also a lot of animals, that's for sure," Max declares.

All eight are excited and nervous at the same time. They are slowly flying over the island.

"There are people there. I can hear talking in several places on the island. I don't know if it's the distance or because they speak their own dialect, but I can't understand a thing they're saying," says Tabitha.

"Look, on this side," says Stephanie, pointing at some kind of shelter.

"Well done, Steph," says Cathy. "They look like temples."

"Tab, can you hear anything there?" asks Cathy.

"It's quiet around the temple," Tabitha replies.

"And besides, there is a beautiful clearing around the temple that seems to be made for our shuttle," says James.

His brow furrows as he concentrates on the difficult landing.

"Now what do we do?" asks Chris. "We haven't even reached our first objective yet. You have a better idea?"

"Are there many people?" Jesse asks Tabitha.

"I'd say maybe two hundred, spread over three places on the island."

"Well, that's not going to be a problem, then."

"Hey, guys, we didn't come here to exterminate the last survivors of the human race," Leah says, arms crossed in front of Jesse.

"Leah, do you realize what this means?" Cathy says. "Isolated people on this island? Can you imagine what we can learn and also what you can bring them? What if, instead of killing them, we thought about saving them?"

"That works for me," Max says.

"And for me too," adds Chris.

"Okay, guys, I'm not going to screw up your friends," Jesse tells them. "But still, we should all come out armed—well-armed."

"Our mission to stay alive, all eight of us, remains our priority," says Tabitha.

"That also works for me," James adds.

"I'm too excited," says Stephanie, who hasn't stopped contemplating the temples.

The shuttle lands gently in a meadow.

"The grass has been cut by people. Look at the jungle around us," James notes.

"Maybe there are shuttles that come here from time to time," Jesse replies.

"Well, I don't think this is a good idea anymore," Chris adds. "And are we going to leave all our stuff here like this?"

"Do you want to stay in the shuttle?" Jesse asks him.

"Come on, stop pulling that face," Cathy says. "It'll do you good to get out."

They're dressing and arming themselves as Jesse advised. Stephanie walks by Chris and puts one hand on his shoulder to reassure him.

"Ooh, lovebirds!" Jesse can't help but shout.

Cathy throws him a punch to the stomach.

"Calm down, Cathy," he replies with a laugh.

"Well, are we ready?" asks Max. "I'm looking forward to getting some fresh air."

"What's the radioactivity level?" James asks Leah.

"All good. We can go out without suits."

James opens one of the shuttle doors and a damp heat immediately hits their faces.

"Wow! Where are we now?" asks Max, his voice excited.

"On an island near the Equator," says Stephanie. "The humidity in these regions is much higher than in our place."

The Eight look at the jungle, the magnificent birds flying above them, and especially the majestic temples, undoubtedly built by man, a long time ago. Pots with flowers placed on several steps show that there is human activity.

"Tab, in which direction do you think we should go?" asks Cathy, who has little interest in temples.

Stephanie and Max stroll to the buildings and touch the treasures.

"Do you realize that these temples are at least one thousand years old, if not more? It's extraordinary!" exclaims Stephanie.

"Come on, let's go," says Jesse.

"I think we should stay here with Stephanie to explore the temples," Max suggests. "We may learn a lot."

"And to keep an eye on the shuttle," Chris adds.

"Yes, let's all three of us stay together," says Stephanie, relieved. "You go find the people. I prefer the stones."

"Okay, that works for me," says Cathy. "How about you, Leah?"

"I'm coming with you to make sure Jesse doesn't kill everyone."

"Ha ha. You better stay close to me, my girlfriend," Jesse replies, holding her hand.

The five of them plunge into the jungle, following Tabitha and Cathy. The two girls are in front, all their senses alert, trying to assess in which direction the nearest human presence is located.

"It really feels good to stretch your legs," says James, who is a few meters behind.

"It's certain that at this rate, staying in the shuttle all the time, we'll get soft," adds Jesse. "And I was getting a little bored."

"Boredom," says Leah. "You're kidding, I hope."

"No, I'm not kidding. We only have ten days until we're back. So far, we spent most of those first few days locked in a plastic and aluminum prison."

"And I still haven't bathed, even though we've seen billions of cubic meters of water," James adds.

"Yeah, but even so boys, look around you right now. We're no longer in the Dome. It's great!" Leah tells them.

"Well, yeah, that's what we say. It was time to go out," grumbles James.

Cathy and Tabitha have stopped walking.

"I would say there are about fifty of them," says Tabitha.

“Get ready,” Cathy tells them. “We’ll go and give them the fright of their lives.”

The five come out of the jungle and arrive in a village of patched-up wooden houses, where men, women, and children, dressed in simple and generally light clothing, engage in various activities.

Children are the first to notice these young strangers, with their unfamiliar clothes and weapons. For all they know, these visitors could have come from another planet. Most of the children look at them with kindness and curiosity, but the younger ones appear frightened and start crying. This immediately attracts the attention of the adults. From that moment on, chaos erupts. Women scream, grab their children to hide them, while the men immediately collect spears and cutlasses and advance in groups towards the strangers.

The five Elites raise their arms as a sign of peace.

“We come in peace,” Cathy shouts at them. “We have come in peace.”

“I don’t understand their language,” Tabitha tells them. “We’re missing Stephanie right now.”

“Does anyone speak our language?” Cathy continues to shout.

“Maybe they won’t talk to a woman,” says Jesse. “Looks like a good macho society to me.” He shouts at them, “Comprende español? Kennen sie deutsch?”

The men talk to each other and quickly one of them brings up an elderly woman and a younger girl and pushes them brusquely towards the Elites.

“Well, I feel like I’m going to like it here.” Cathy can feel the animosity, the anguish of the inhabitants, but especially the fear of all towards the men who brought the old woman.

"Do you speak our language?" asks Leah to both women, with all the gentleness she can muster.

"Yes, we talk a little," replies the elderly woman. "My mother spoke it, and I passed it on to my daughter and then my granddaughter here."

Leah looks at the girl. She looks scared. "You mustn't be afraid of us, my little one."

"She's not afraid of you, she's afraid of them. They think we are witches to speak your language. We're going to pay dearly for it afterward."

Indeed, behind them, the men are agitated and shouting at the two women words that the five do not understand.

"They want to know where you come from and what you're doing here."

"Tell them we're going to another island further away and we'll leave soon. We just have a few questions," offers Leah.

The woman translates the answer into their dialect, but the evil looks remain.

"I'm going to have trouble controlling myself. Do you see how these men behave?" Cathy telepaths to her friends.

"Calm down and take your time, Cathy. Evaluate the different profiles carefully. Let's not act in a hurry," James replies.

"Cathy, I've entered the minds of a few guys in front of me. They're total creeps," adds Jesse.

"I'm ready," Tabitha adds.

Leah turns to look at all four with a reprimand.

"What do you know about the Ecological Wars?" she asks the two women.

At that moment, a man violently pushes the girl to the ground.

Leah throws herself forward to catch her and gets kicked as well.

The anger that had been building inside Cathy since she arrived in the village explodes.

"Let's start with this one," she tells Tabitha.

"Then this one on the right," she says to James.

"And the very tall one with the weird head," she says to Jesse.

Cathy continues to give orders to the other three. Each of them eliminates the target designated by their friend with a single shot. Those who try to escape are directly shot by Cathy.

All the villagers are now either on the ground or being brought back to the middle of the village by Jesse, Tabitha, and James. Leah is sitting, holding the two women in her arms.

"Have you lost your mind?" she shouts at Cathy, who comes back in her direction.

"I need her," she replies, pointing to the elderly woman.

"No, you've really lost it!" screams Leah.

"What do you want?" asks the woman, getting up painfully.

"I want to know if the whole village is there and if I forgot one of the bastards."

Tabitha and Jesse have everyone in their sights while they continue to survey the area. James, for his part, brings back all the bodies, about fifteen or so, and puts them all next to each other, in plain view.

The old lady takes her time, walks through the crowd of villagers gathered, says something to everyone. Her words have the immediate effect of calming the crying and their fear. Then she points to a young man hiding behind the children. He begins to run towards the jungle. But Cathy doesn't have time to lift her gun; he falls dead, under Leah's bullet. The two friends look at each other, a shared pain in their eyes.

"Tell them that they have nothing to fear anymore," says Cathy to the old woman.

There is now a great silence in the center of the village.

"That's what I've already told them because you're like the white man who saved our people."

The five Elites have noted the old lady's words well. A great curiosity animates their eyes.

"Let's clean that up first," says Cathy, pointing to the bodies.

A strong smell begins to emanate, as the heat is high and humid.

"After that, I think you have a story to tell us," she adds.

The elderly woman began to give orders in her dialect. Men and women come to help James carry the bodies and take them to a place that they apparently use as a cemetery. Others sprinkle water on the ground where blood has been shed, permanently eliminating traces of battle. Finally, the youngest and oldest gather a little further into the village, around a statue representing a good and almighty god.

Barely half an hour has passed and the whole village and the five Elites are now gathered around the statue.

The elderly woman begins her story, while the young girl translates into her dialect to the rest of the audience:

"A long time ago, in my grandmother's time, a white man arrived on the island. He was very tall, very thin, with big blue-gray eyes. My people used to see white people passing through the island. But this one was different. He didn't ask for anything. He just wanted to live with our people. He was good and helped everyone in the community. And then one day, he told them that a great disaster was about to happen and that it was necessary to build shelters under the temples and to store provisions for several years. The villagers had a lot of respect for him, so they listened to him. A few weeks passed and one day he told them all to go underground to safety. Most of them followed him, but some preferred to stay outside. After a while, they heard many unknown noises and then silence. My grandmother often talked to me about this silence, as if nothing was living outside anymore. The white man ordered them to stay as long as they could, and they stayed under the temples for months until there was no food left. When they came out, everything they had known no longer existed, as if a huge hurricane had blown everything away. They relearned to live in this new environment, with life and nature taking back their rights.

"My grandmother already had a daughter, and the white man began to live with them. And when I was born, I also stayed with them. That's how I learned your language, and my granddaughter knows it too."

"But then what happened that you had so many cruel and vicious men with you today?" asks Cathy.

"When I was a child and the white man was still here, he had proposed rules of life that worked for the good of everyone. Everyone helped each other and got along. And then when he died, everything went wrong. It started with simple quarrels, jealousies, and then gradually some men wanted more power and privileges."

Her eyes are clouded for an instant as she stares off into the distance.

"My daughter was very beautiful. Several men coveted her, but she was not interested in them. One day, men from the nearby village, a little further into the jungle, kidnapped her for several days. When she returned, she was no longer the same. Months later, she gave birth to my granddaughter."

She interrupts her speech, to catch her breath and struggle past the painful memory.

"The next day, she got up and walked into the sea."

Leah, like the others in the assembly, has tears in her eyes.

"We have all lived in terror these last ten years. There are other bad seeds in the other two villages. Some are even women.

The old woman now also has tears in her eyes.

"How can I thank you? You're like the white man and you're saving us again."

"This white man," asks Tabitha. "Did he have anything that made him stand out? Anything recognizable?"

"Yes, absolutely. He had a sign on his left shoulder blade. He called it the Mark."

The Elites are now marching towards the second village. Some men and women wanted to accompany them, to serve as guides and to see the show. The girl accompanies them to be their interpreter.

"I'm sorry, Cathy, for doubting you," Leah says.

"Don't worry, my friend, we went very hard and very fast, but I felt such horrible things in them."

"How can men become like that?

"Do you still think men are good, Leah?" asks Tabitha. "The human race has killed, slaughtered and destroyed everything that can be destroyed. And even in a very small society like this, it barely takes a few generations for some people to become monstrous again. They form packs, take pleasure in terrorizing others, just to increase their power. I can tell you that I look forward to exterminating them. But we should take our time this time. Boys, you leave them to us."

"Oh! There are also women, apparently," Jesse answers.

"And not all men are like them," James says, evidently feeling the sting.

"What fascinates me is that the famous white man had the Mark and that he knew what was going to happen. That's interesting," adds Jesse thoughtfully.

"Well, I'm interested in killing all these bastards," Cathy says. "You have no idea what I've seen and felt in some people's heads."

She looks at James.

"Yes, not all men are like that," she says. "Maybe that's why you have the Mark. Like the white man who was good. Like you."

"And who knew what was going to happen?" Jesse says thoughtfully.

"What's your new theory of the day then?" Tabitha asks.

"At first I thought it was because we were superheroes."

The four friends immediately start laughing.

"Or we were chosen and marked at birth."

"Oh, yeah, and by a god, too," Tabitha adds.

Jesse continues without addressing her.

"But perhaps we are simply descendants of those men who were chosen to survive the Apocalypse."

"Stephanie will love that," Tabitha says with a mocking tone.

Jesse and Stephanie enjoy discussing this subject.

"We'll see what she has to say about the white man's story, says Jesse. "First, we have a job to do. We have arrived. Girls, have fun!"

The group has arrived in the village. This one is a little smaller than the previous one, but a similar hustle and bustle exists here too. However, everything stops when the villagers finally notice the startling presence of the Elites among them. Their guides engage in a lively discussion, punctuated by the screams and cries of the women and children.

"Do you see any monsters, Cathy?" ask Leah.

"No, not at the moment."

"Be careful, there are people coming," says Tabitha.

A dozen men and women of all ages walk in their direction. They do not seem surprised by their presence. Someone must have managed to escape from the other village and warned them. They are all armed. Rudimentary weapons, of course, but they clearly took everything they had. Everyone has at least a club or a knife. Some hold bows and arrows, already aimed at the Elites. Their faces are distorted by rage and madness.

"Oh, good. That would have been too easy and really not fun," Jesse laughs.

"Come on, girls, make us proud," James adds. "They all look like real bastards."

Leah, Tabitha, and Cathy quickly give the boys their guns, and nonchalantly move towards the crowd.

The three eighteen-year-old girls look impressive: Leah, the little redhead, Cathy, the blonde with green eyes and long hair, and Tabitha, tall and beautiful, with her black eyes and dark skin. They stand in front of them with their arms crossed.

"So, Cathy, what are they like?" asks Leah.

"Oh, yes, very horrible. Rapists, perverts."

"Let's get them," Tabitha says with a big smile.

The girls start running together and throw themselves onto the crowd. This is followed by a martial arts ballet. There are three or four opponents for each of the girls. Yet the men's excited roars quickly give way to cries of pain, then to silence.

The boys join the three girls to help them finish the job.

Even the birds have stopped chirping.

"They definitely think we are monsters," says Leah, appalled by her own show of violence.

"That's kind of what we are, aren't we?" asks Cathy.

"Yes. We were trained to become monsters," says James, who has stopped and is now watching all four of them.

"Right now, we're finishing the job," says Jesse. "We get rid of their own monsters. We, the other monsters, will leave later."

James pulls four bodies a little further away from the village and the children.

When they have finished their cleaning, all five of them come back to the village. There is still the same silence.

Cathy goes to see their young interpreter.

"Tell them that it will be better for them and that all the bad men and women who were violent and evil will be eliminated from the island. And that they can and must now live in peace and help each other."

Everyone is shedding tears.

"I think they are a little shocked by what has just happened," says the girl, after translating to the people of the village.

"Let's get going," Cathy replies.

The group resumes its journey to the third and smallest village. The girl tells them that she thinks there may be one or two deviant people in this village, but she is not sure. They live far from others for this reason.

"She is sincere," says Cathy. "Let's go anyway."

"Let's hurry, "Jesse says, "and then join the others at the temples."

The village is only a few minutes' walk away and the group is going at a good pace. When they arrive, their guides, once again, first talk to the villagers. The screams and cries follow. Cathy inspects everyone and Tabitha tries to find those who are hiding. Cathy shakes her head.

Leah exhales in relief.

"Let's go quickly to the temples," orders Cathy.

They are all running towards the temples that seem to be in the center of the island, which is surprisingly small. They are all astonished to find the elderly woman in a deep discussion with Stephanie, Max, and Chris.

"It's fascinating," says Stephanie

"And the white man had the Mark. Too cool," Max adds.

"Oh, yeah?" says Leah, sulking. "We just killed a lot of people. Just like that. That's not so cool. I should have stayed with you."

Max takes her in his arms in a protective gesture.

"It's for the good of the whole community," Cathy tells her.

Leah snaps. "Do you think we have the right to come here and decide for them?"

"Perverts, child rapists, men who beat women," Cathy says. "What would you have done then?"

"I can't believe there's no other way but to kill them."

Tabitha intervenes, addressing the elderly woman. "Ma'am, you absolutely must educate boys to respect women. That is the key to everything," she says authoritatively. "This must be done from an early age and must be reinforced throughout their lives."

"For this generation and those to come, we will tell them that if they don't behave well, you will come back!" answers the old woman.

She starts laughing, showing her toothless grin

"New norms of gender relations must be put in place," Tabitha continues. "Otherwise, it will happen again. Men will regain control, and will use violence to assert their dominance. You need men for procreation, and to protect you, yes, but don't underestimate yourself. A good community and mutual support among women can replace the strength of men and not force you into submission."

She turns around to Cathy and grabs her arm. "It was really the right thing to do."

"Yes, it was the right thing to do," Max adds. I don't even understand how some men can do such horrors. In our world, no one would behave like that."

"Are you sure about that?" Ask Jesse.

"You can criticize the Red World as you wish, and you know how critical I am, but this kind of violence was eradicated a long time ago," Max answers.

"A solid point for the Red World," concedes Cathy.

They finally decide to stay the evening on the island to avoid traveling at night over the ocean.

The elderly woman invites them into the village. Their hosts obviously made a lot of effort to serve them a royal feast. The meal is made of food that they have barely heard about. The Eight discover fruits that they thought had disappeared forever, such as juicy orange-colored mangos, or bananas, fleshy but sweet and bitter at the same time. Nature seems to have been preserved here more than anywhere else. Stephanie says it's because they're at a point far enough away from the nuclear power plants, which had exploded all over the world in 2025.

After the meal, the islanders beguile the visitors with traditional music and songs. From time to time, they stop dancing and then an elderly person starts telling a traditional story about nature, men, wars, and then the white man. The Eight follow all this with great attention. Life here seems so different to theirs, so close to nature.

As the hours go by, the children are less afraid of them, especially Leah and Max. They soon find themselves dancing with the villagers, and Max's frantic dancing steps are greeted with laughter.

Within a few hours, joy has replaced fear and despair.

Later that night, they leave the village to sleep in their shuttle.

"Don't you find it surprising that the leaders of the Red World, proud descendants of men who spent their lives exploring and creating the great empires, did not come here to exploit the raw materials?" wonders Stephanie out loud, voicing what the others are obviously thinking.

"This would improve life in Kantas City," Chris adds.

"Less than a day by plane," Cathy chimes in.

"The food is too good," exclaims James.

"Ms. Know-It-All, we are waiting for your theory!" Jesse says to Stephanie.

"So," she says after considering, "if our leaders traveled the world twenty-five years ago like we are doing, or even if they are only aware that there are such places where nature has regained its rights, and yet they do not send shuttles, then it is out of an anti-empirical will. It's a reaction to the history before the Ecological Wars.

"Can we get a translation for that?" asks Cathy.

"The empire was the most common form of political organization in the last 2500 years before the destruction of their world in 2025. These empires were maintained through war and oppression in general. Perhaps our Founders decided that we should not start invading and colonizing the world again. Everyone stays in our Red World."

"Yes, but hey, those bananas were too good!" adds James

"Ach, James," Cathy says to him with a smile.

"As for me, I'm going to sleep in the temples!" says Max to them.

James and Jesse team up to bring him back into the shuttle.

SOMEWHERE IN INDONESIA, 2025, BART

------------ *Adrien, "underground", 2027*
------------ *Indigo, Paris, 2025*
------------ *Fadi, Egypt, 2025*
------------ *Bart, Indonesia, 2025*
------------ *Sarah, United States, 2022*
------------ *Anna, Lascaux, France, 2006*

BART WAKES UP SUDDENLY, as he has done every night in recent months, and touches his scar. It hurts him more and more, revealing that it will finally happen. And then the odor of dampness coupled with that of dried flowers reaches him and a great feeling of serenity invades his senses.

"I'm exactly where I need to be."

He had been surveying the borders of the Indonesian islands for years on behalf of an NGO funded by the Dutch government, and he knew the islands like the back of his hand. He had chosen this island for the thousand-year-old temples, built on natural cellars, more solid than concrete shelters. But also for the population, who lived quietly and humbly in the pure Buddhist tradition.

"They deserve to be saved," he says aloud to himself, to justify his decision.

He knows that his colleagues must be looking for him right now, but it's like looking for a needle in a haystack; there are so many islands and places to hide. And this island is particularly unknown and outside the circuits, whether humanitarian or tourist.

Some of them must be furious in Amsterdam, that's for sure. At this idea, a feeling of contentment, but also of rage, invades him. How did the human race reach such a level of destruction?

And then, he wonders, all alone in the dark, if the real reason for choosing this island, is not simply the young woman with almond-shaped eyes who had welcomed him on the beach where she was quietly collecting wood. She had looked at him with a surprised look when he appeared in his small boat. She had gone to meet him. Her dark and deep look had captivated him. Her smile had finally claimed his heart. Since then, his only desire has been to continue seeing that face.

"Yes, that's how I'm going to save the world! By falling in love!"

He's trying to go back to sleep. Tomorrow, he will have a lot of work to do. Dig, patch, and prepare the shelters. And he needs to go even faster. The Mark reminds him. The end of the world is about to happen.

CHAPTER 15

IN THE VALLEY

Day 6 of the trip, year 2125

THEY LEAVE AT DAWN.

Stephanie, Chris, and Max are writing down and drawing everything they have seen, learned, or tasted during their stay on the island when they arrive over a larger island that seems to be their destination. They are speeding as quickly as possible to reach the coordinates given by Zeus.

They reach a pretty little hill covered with greenery, near a beach. Excitement and expectation are felt throughout the shuttle. Why did Zeus send them here? What is there in this place, on the other side of the world?

"There, in front of us. I feel human activity," says Tabitha.

"Where? We can't see anything," says James, as he flies the shuttle toward the place Tabitha points out.

Everyone else presses their faces to the windows to see where humans might be hiding.

"I sense it too," says Cathy, "but I can't see anything."

"It's beautiful here," exclaims Leah.

"What if they're underground?" suggests Jesse.

"We're going to land and find them," says James, who is beginning the descent.

"Come on, everybody! Get your weapons," says Cathy.

"Yes, chances are we won't be greeted with bananas," Max adds.

Everyone laughs, but nervously.

As they leave the shuttle, the pure and fresh air surprises them all. They start inhaling deeply and a soft cleanliness fills their lungs.

"What is it?" asks Max.

"Normal air, not shitty air," answers Jesse.

"Wow, that's great. I've decided. I'll stay here. Just to breathe."

"Well, I'm sorry to break it to you, but, you're coming back with us."

"Guys, let me take a swim. I can't see the sea looking so inviting and not go in," begs James.

"Come on, let's all go," Cathy suggests.

They all start running towards the sea. Excitement has replaced apprehension.

"You guys go ahead, my friends," Leah suggests. "Go into the water and I'll keep your clothes and weapons. It would be a shame to lose everything."

"Okay, I'll take the next turn," Cathy tells her.

They descend a steep hillside to reach a small cove surrounded by steep rocks. When they finally arrive, they take off all their clothes and dive into the water. The water is salty and this surprises them. It gently surrounds them. Rather cold, it slightly pricks their skin. *It's so different from our pools in Kantas City,* they all think.

After a while, Stephanie and Cathy get out to give Leah a chance to soothe her body in this pure water.

"It's amazing, Leah. Get in quickly," Cathy says to her.

"Look at James, he's waving. He's found something."

James has already swum several kilometers over and under the water, and in a few strokes, returns to his friends.

"He came to get Tabitha," Cathy says.

He takes Tabitha on his back and brings her at full speed a little further along the coast. They both dive several times. Meanwhile, the others are waiting for them at the cove.

James is taking Tabitha back to their friends.

"We found where they are," Tabitha tells them.

"When I dived, I found several entrances to underground cellars," James says. "Incredible technology, with iron doors."

"Are they fish men, or what?" asks Max, while shaking his long, curly hair.

"Maybe. We'll see," James answers. "I was also able to see a well-hidden staircase above the underground entrances."

"Great, let's go check it out!" exclaims Cathy. "Take Leah with you, James. You can swim there and we'll get dressed and walk across with your stuff and weapons. Tabitha will guide us."

James and Leah immediately swim away while the others go up the small hill.

Tabitha takes them to where the stairs should be.

Chris runs to the shuttle to get his "gear," as he calls his computers and other instruments.

When he returns, he discovers what he believes to be an ingenious system to hide the staircase which is embedded in the rock

"Look! There are cameras. Everyone say 'Hello,'" jokes Jesse.

Cathy takes the lead of the small troop and runs down the stairs. James and Leah climb the rock to join them, in front of what seems to be a door.

"Put your clothes on, young people, or you're going to shock our future friends, who must be watching us," Jesse says in a playful tone. "Even if you look quite good, Leah."

"I remind you that we were all naked a few minutes ago, so our anatomy is now well known," Max adds. "And I'm still the hottest."

"Stop joking around kids. Can't you help Chris and me open the door instead?" Stephanie tells them.

"If you both can't do it, I don't see why we mere idiots are going to be able to do it," Jesse answers.

Suddenly, from an invisible speaker, a voice calls out: "Who are you?"

"My name is Cathy."

"My name is Jesse."

"And I'm Max, and next to me is James, Tabitha, Stephanie, Chris, and Leah."

"What do you want?" asks the voice.

"I don't know, maybe I could play music," Max says.

"Stop it," Cathy says, smiling. "Seriously, someone has given us your geographical coordinates so we can meet you."

"We don't want to meet you," the voice replies.

"You see Max, it's because of your anatomy, that's for sure," Jesse tells him.

"Well, if you don't want to see me, I'll go back and swim," James says.

"Bingo," exclaims Chris.

"You're really too good," Cathy says, rushing into the entrance. "Quick, the masks!" she shouts.

Smoke comes out on either side of the corridor into which they are rushing. Max and Leah stay back to block the exit door and prevent everyone from being trapped in this corridor. Another door is a few dozen meters in front of them.

"It's an armored door, and there is a code system. I need a few minutes but it should be pretty easy to unlock," says Chris, who is resuming telepathic communication.

"I think there are about a hundred people behind it," adds Tabitha. *"And they seem to be very, very afraid."*

"Fear will make them dangerous," Cathy says. *"But let's try not to shoot, okay?"*

"Do you want me to be the negotiator?" suggests Jesse.

"Oh, sure," Cathy replies. *"Leah, you're going to try to calm them down, okay?"*

On the other side, the cameras only see a small, brown-skinned young man typing on a computer and a redheaded girl, who walked towards the entrance, followed by a huge blond fellow.

"I'm protecting her," James tells them.

"Yes, watch out for her," Chris replies. *"Get ready, the door will open in five, four, three, two, one.... Now!"*

With a loud creak, the mechanism slowly opens the door, to reveal to the Elites the presence of about thirty armed men and women facing them, ready to fire.

Leah walks towards them slowly, hands out as a sign of peace.

"Don't be afraid, we come in peace. We'd just like to talk to you."

"Then why are you prepared for combat?" asks a young man with a deep voice.

"It's only been a few days since we left where we came from, and we don't really know who we're going to meet. My friend behind me, who's called Cathy, can read people's minds. And if she says you're not bad guys, we're all going to put our guns down, okay?"

"Bad guys, are you kidding?" replies the young man. "You break in here, and we're the bad guys?"

"Cathy?" asks Leah, in her quietest voice.

"At the very least, they're no worse than us. It's okay, guys, we can do it."

And all seven come forward after laying down their arms.

"It's your turn to lower your weapons," says Leah. "We come in peace."

"We have already met eight young men and women, dressed a little like you. They came here twenty-five years ago, and the meeting was not the nicest. So why should we trust you any more than them?"

The Elites look at each other with bewilderment.

"Because they were real bad guys. We know them well, and we don't like them either. We are different," says Leah.

The men and women in front of them still don't move.

"They are afraid," Tabitha says. "Really, really afraid."

"We didn't come here to hurt you," says Leah. "We can even help you. For example, I know how to heal people. If someone is sick in your home, I can cure them."

Still no movement.

"Our parents," Jesse and Tabitha say, telepathically.

"It was Zeus who gave us these geographical coordinates, and yet the former Elite students have already come. Weird, right?" adds Max.

"They keep manipulating us in Kantas City," says Cathy angrily.

"Cathy, do you know who to talk to?" asks Leah.

"Yes, I think so," Cathy replies.

And Cathy addresses them:

"You're all very intelligent people, there's no doubt about that. If some of you remember those who came here twenty-five years ago, you should know that some of them were bastards and that we are not like them. But if you thought they were very strong and dangerous, know that we are even stronger than they are. With our weapons, much more sophisticated than yours, and our training, we could kill you all in minutes. Either you trust us, or we exterminate you."

"That was a hell of a negotiation," says Jesse sarcastically.

A minute passes. Nobody moves.

The young man who had spoken earlier stares at Cathy. She is trying to access his mind, but to her great surprise, without success. They both look at each other for several seconds, but to Cathy it feels like several minutes have passed. Finally, the voice they had heard outside begins to resonate throughout the room.

"The kid is right. Put down your weapons."

The men and women in front of them gently lay down their weapons. Some show through their facial expressions that they do not necessarily agree with the voice.

The Eight are now all lined up in front of the group and waiting to see what happens next. They note the genetic mix of men and women as a mirror of their own small group.

"Impressive. It could be us," Cathy says telepathically.

"Pay attention, the leaders are coming," says Tabitha.

About ten people who seem to be between forty and sixty years old are walking in their direction. Some of them must be the parents of those who hold the guns.

A tall woman, with black skin and laughing, intelligent eyes, walks towards them. "Hello, Elite students. We've been waiting for you."

"Thank you, but how did you know we were coming?" asks Leah, who has resumed her role as negotiator and is now acting naïvely.

"It seems that we are part of your learning because we receive your visits exactly every twenty-five years. So, we always get ready for you. But our technology seems quite outdated compared to yours. None of the other Eight Elite student groups has ever entered so quickly and easily," she says, staring at Chris, visibly intrigued by the extent of his knowledge.

"What is strange is that we got your geographical coordinates from one of the main Rebel leaders. Those are the one fighting against the Government of our world. They're made up of the Eight who came to see you last time," says Jesse.

"There are lots of reasons to rebel if those previous visitors now form your Government," she says with a hint of bitterness in her voice.

"How do you manage not to have psychopaths or other violent people in your group?" asks Cathy, who has never stopped studying the growing crowd.

The woman replies simply, pointing to the people around her.

"We are a group of very intelligent people, fair and with a very good moral sense."

"And strong personalities that are difficult to control," Jesse adds.

Jesse has tried to get into the minds of some of the people in front of him, including the one who has spoken to them, but with no success.

"The answer to your question, Cathy, is that we are obliged to ask them to leave because we do not have the appropriate structures to help them."

She adds, "I'm Michelle, by the way. One last thing, you are welcome to stay here with us for a few days. You're either here to assist or destroy us. Either way, it will have consequences for the next twenty-five years, for both of us."

The Eight look at each other.

"Cathy, what do we do?" asks James telepathically.

"They have about the same level of ethics and morality as we do," Cathy says. *"It's worth taking the time to get to know them."*

"It's a little weird to get so close to them so fast, but what are our choices?" asks Tabitha.

"Considering all the options, this is the best one," says Stephanie. *"Earn their trust and learn about them."*

"Be careful. They are very intelligent so let's remain vigilant," Jesse concludes.

All of them appoint Max to be their spokesman.

"Thank you, Michelle. Of course, you see us, like everyone else, as Elite students, who have been trained to fight, kill, and lead—which we do very well. But when you get to know us better and individually, you will understand that we are above all thirsty for knowledge, freedom, and experiences. It is obvious that we want to collaborate and share our knowledge with you."

Michelle's eyes glisten and everyone feels her relief immediately transmitted to the rest of her group.

Encouraged by her response Max continues.

"We will be frank with you. Each of us has developed certain faculties that are superior to the other members of our group. I, for example...."

Tabitha interrupts him immediately.

"Are you sure you know what you're doing, Max? We never talk about it with anyone else. Why start now?"

"Tabitha, if we want to earn their trust, we must put some cards on the table."

Cathy eyes Max with an intense but uncertain look. Finally, she decides to speak first.

"My name is Cathy, and I can read people's faces and detect their degree of morality and depth of character. That's why I trust you fully."

"And I'm Leah. I have the gift of diagnosing and treating diseases."

"I'm Stephanie. My memory is immense and I am very smart."

"It's true, she is," adds Chris. "And I'm pretty good at computers and anything else that has buttons."

"Yes, he's a real star," Max adds. "I can talk to animals. Yeah, I know, it's weird. They talk back to me, too. And also, I'm pretty cool with musical instruments."

"My name is James. I was born big and strong, and I swim like an eel."

“Okay, I’m Tabitha. I often seem unhappy but I can hear everything from far away. Like you in the orange shirt telling your friend you think I’m hot.”

The whole assembly starts laughing, which swiftly warms the atmosphere.

“I didn’t know you had a sense of humor, sweetheart. I’m Jesse, and I’m the least cool of the gang. I can access someone’s brain and force them to do what I want. But I promise I won’t play that little game with you!”

“Welcome,” Michelle says with a big smile. “I can see that we are going to spend a few interesting days together.”

She approaches Leah and takes her in her arms. Those next to them do the same. The Elites are not used to such a warm welcome and respond clumsily to the hugs. All of them introduce themselves with first names that are as diverse as they are unique.

Michelle leads them out of what now seems like a very small and simple entrance, next to the main living space. What they see takes their breath away.

“Wow, that’s amazing,” says Stephanie.

“What beautiful colors!” exclaims Max.

“It’s big and bright, but most of all it’s amazing that we didn’t see anything from outside,” adds Chris.

Michelle says, “Our ancestors installed the most advanced technology of their time, but that was more than a hundred years ago.”

The Eight advance towards the essential element of the room: a six-story-high glass wall about sixty meters wide, completely invisible from the outside, and appearing to be an ordinary rock face. It allows in natural light while giving the impression of being outside, and has a magnificent view of the ocean.

"I'll stay here," sighs James, who cannot take his eyes off the sea in front of him.

A young man, named Zayn, who could have been Chris' older brother, answers his questions before he can ask.

"It is an illusion," he says. "Images that we project. We have triple glazing, which is sufficient when the weather is normal as it is today. But our site was built to be a fallout shelter. The panel there closes and we find ourselves in a box. We are under the hill, and partially under the sea."

"Our ancestors survived like this for a few years before they could get out," Michelle adds. "And even then, our part of the world had not been affected as much."

"Yes, we were surprised by the clean air when we arrived here," says Stephanie.

"It's very pleasant outdoors, but we limit our outings. Another topic for discussion later," Michelle says, evasively.

"We look forward to having that conversation," Jesse adds.

Michelle looks at him with a smirk on her face.

"Come on, I'll show you around. We call this place 'the Valley.'"

"Is that another interesting conversation?" Jesse asks.

Michelle doesn't answer.

The rest of the Valley's inhabitants have returned to their usual activities, but everyone looks at the Elites with great interest every time they pass by. Michelle and Zayn introduce them as they go along. They show them where the different dwellings and common areas are. They walk through a large room where children and young people are studying. Books are spread on shelves around them. Stephanie refrains from rushing to them.

"You will soon get to go," Chris says to her. "Just a few more minutes."

"Unfortunately, your predecessors eliminated some of them," Michelle tells him. There is a touch of anger in her voice.

"Yet another conversation, right?" says James.

Michelle just looks at him smiling. She also shows them where they produce food, where they do their sports and "personal development," as they call it; where the technical section with servers and batteries is located; where all the products that can no longer be manufactured are stored, from mattresses to light bulbs, notebooks, pencils, etc.

"Your ancestors were very far-sighted," Tabitha notes.

"Yes, but for only 150 years," Michelle tells them. "And that's the problem. We have started to make some adjustments, but still, time passes quickly and we are limited in space. By that I mean the exploration space around the Valley."

"Well, I'd like to have this conversation," Jesse says.

Michelle looks at them all in turn, hesitating, then suggests, "Why don't we take a walk outside?"

She dismisses those who accompany her, except Zayn, a young woman named Tiff, and the young man with the deep voice, named Tom. He was the one who had first spoken to them, and who had since followed the group, but at a reasonable distance and with an air of defiance. He is very tall, thin, with blond hair turning red, with an emaciated face and slightly sunken green eyes. He must be just a few years older than the Elites. The young woman named Tiff is also about the same age and exudes common sense and intelligence. *Another Stephanie,* Cathy thinks to herself. *She, too, is a tall brunette. Almost my clone.*

The group takes an elevator, then another staircase that leads to another trapdoor, this time directly to the surface and absolutely undetectable to the untrained eye.

Once again, the Eight can't help but take a deep breath.

"Is it still so polluted where you come from?" asks Zayn.

"We can get out of the Dome that covers our city now, but it is nothing like here," says Chris.

"In fact, we passed a completely destroyed area where the levels of radiation were incredibly high as if an atomic bomb had just been detonated," adds Stephanie.

"If you want, we can look together in the library. It could give us some interesting information," suggests Tiff.

"That would be great. We are always looking for information about the past," she answers.

An immediate connection is created between the two girls and they are already sharing what they read, what is in the library or in the Red World.

Cathy and Leah look at each other with smiles on their faces. Stephanie seems so happy to meet someone who shares the same interests as her.

Tabitha and Jesse walk a little behind the group and talk to each other. Chris explains to Zayn the latest technologies available in the shuttle. Leah, Max, James, and Michelle discuss the surrounding nature and its biodiversity, while Cathy stays just behind Tom, trying to assess the complexity of his character. But as she had noticed before, Tom has a very strong personality and is difficult to read.

Chris guides them and brings them closer to their shuttle. He enters quickly to come out just as quickly with a box that his friends know well.

"Now you can talk to us with complete peace of mind. This listening jammer will prevent any known technology from following our conversation."

"Chris is right, we felt your reluctance to talk to us. Is it because of us or something else?" Cathy asks.

"I hope you are right about that jammer, because it is possible that people will try and listen to us. But the other reason is that I preferred not to talk to you in the presence of our friends below. The situation is difficult for everyone."

The eight friends are now clinging to her words as they walk towards a small hill.

"Our ancestors were very rich people. Among the richest on the planet, and they had built these shelters in the event of a natural disaster or war. They spent more than fifteen years working on it."

"Are there others or just this one?" asks James.

"According to our ancestors, there are several of them on this island, and they are quite close," says Tiff. "And also on the continent where they came from."

"And where did they come from?" asks Stephanie, who cannot contain her excitement.

"They were from California, in the United States. From a place they called Silicon Valley. And now we are on an island that was part of New Zealand," Zayn tells them.

"We were right," declares Stephanie.

"Right about what? Michelle asks.

"New Zealand," replies Stephanie. "We no longer have accurate maps of the world before, but not all the books have been eliminated, so by deduction..."

"By the way, what is this obsession you guys have about destroying everything?" Interrupts Tom, who is speaking again for the first time.

"It's to avoid references to the old world because it could encourage subversive ideas," Cathy replies promptly.

"Cathy, it was the men of the old world who destroyed everything. Conversely, we are trying not to destroy the planet a second time," Tabitha tells her.

"In any case, it's difficult for us to access anything, so I'm looking forward to going for a walk in your library with Tiff," adds Stephanie.

"So, these limited outings, what's the story? Because with what I see in front of me, I wouldn't be able to help but go exploring. It's absolutely magnificent."

They have arrived at the top of the hill. On the other side, a breathtaking scene appears. The weather is particularly clear, and they can see small mountains with rivers that flow into lakes with blue-green reflections. Everything is green and animals walk quietly, indifferent to the humans who gaze down upon them. Everything is so quiet, so idyllic.

"Our ancestors had to stay in the shelter for years before they could come out," Michelle tells them. "And then, of course, they wanted to create an expedition to find other shelters, or simply see what had survived in the country."

"Unfortunately, they didn't make it past one mile around us. Helicopters came to shoot them," Tom adds.

"Of course, others have tried since," says Zayn. "But they never came back."

"Apart from the Eight Elite students we see every twenty-five years, we have had no contact with other humans," Michelle tells them.

"And that's why we're so happy to see you," adds Tiff with a big smile.

"I wonder where the people who shot you came from—certainly not from very far away, and certainly not from our place. Our planes can patrol a few hundred kilometers around the Red World, but we are thousands of kilometers from there," says Jesse.

"Local people with the same technology?" asks James. "Tab, have you ever heard of this from your mother?"

"She always told me there were a few places populated by human beings. But according to her, no society as sophisticated as the Red World," she replies.

"And yet members of the current Government came here twenty-five years ago," James adds. "They must have heard the same story."

Michelle gives Tabitha a questioning look, while she quickly turns her face away.

"What were the other Elite students like?" Max asks to quickly change the subject. "We have our own legends, but I'm curious to hear your version of them."

"The first ones who came seventy-five years ago were celebrated like heroes," says Michelle. "Can you imagine? Our ancestors used to fly all over the world in their private jets and then they find themselves stuck underground for years, while any attempt to explore beyond the kilometer is doomed to failure. When they saw the first eight eighteen-year-olds, they took it as an incredible opportunity and the chance to join your world."

"I guess they had a shuttle like ours," says Chris.

"And they tried to bring some of your people, didn't they?" asks Leah.

"Yes, and they were immediately surrounded by the same helicopters and shuttles," Tom replies.

"To answer your question, Max," says Michelle, "the first Eight Elite students were apparently very curious about the old world because they had only known the Red World and seemed to have received little information about the world before. They were good, Max—like the ones who came twenty-five years later. They shared a lot of information and had to leave a few days after."

"And then there were the others twenty-five years ago, who were not as good, right?" asks Jesse.

"Yes, that's right," Michelle says. "Some of them absolutely wanted to eliminate all traces of the old world. They were particularly aggressive and treated us as their slaves."

"Some?" Jesse asks. "What does that mean?"

"They did not all agree and argued a lot with each other. They didn't have the same vision. Some of them wanted to leave quickly. Others, on the other hand, wanted to spend time with us, to share knowledge."

Michelle stops for a moment, lost in her thoughts.

"They didn't stay long after all," she adds. "But twenty-four hours of their presence had a profound impact on all of us, some more than others."

Her eyes are filled with emotion as she speaks.

"We don't come with the same intentions," says Leah gently stroking her arm.

"As you have probably gathered, they are now the head of the Red World Government," Cathy adds. "But the weird thing, as we've already told you, is that they didn't give us your geographical coordinates."

"Oh yes, a Rebel leader, right?" asks Tom.

"Yes, called Zeus," Cathy replies.

"A god, interesting," Tom replies sarcastically.

Cathy looks at Leah in a way that tells her that she still doesn't understand what this boy's problem is and that he is annoying her.

Leah rolls her eyes in amusement.

"We had never heard of the Rebels," Michelle adds. "They did not exist, at least during the first two meetings with the Elites."

"Yes, it must have started about twenty years ago, if you think about your mother," says Tabitha.

Cathy doesn't react but James can't help but interrupt, "Perhaps it is only related to the mediocrity of our current Government."

"Touché," replies Jesse for Tabitha. "As you can see, Michelle, we too have our questions. We were raised to be the perfect Elites, and despite that, we are friends with the Rebels."

"It seems like a hell of a mess where you're from," Tom tells them, with a big smile.

"Yes, that's true. First and foremost, we lack resources, and that creates tensions," says Stephanie.

"That's what they tell us, Stephanie. That's what they tell us," Chris says to her.

"Why they would throw so many people out of our city doesn't make sense. It only feeds the Rebel camps," says Stephanie.

"Or maybe they have another twisted plan," Jesse adds.

"Do you think your Rebels are preparing a war or something?"

"That's what our Government thinks," James replies. "But so far, there have not been any terrorist acts. They step aside and try to regroup."

"They also accumulate knowledge and strategic information," adds Chris.

"It is true that from what we have seen in Toledo, they are not yet up to the task. Do you think they are, Jesse?" says Tabitha.

"No, but that's because I'm so strong," Jesse laughs.

"Toledo is the closest city to Kantas City," James adds. "That was four days ago and we met many Rebels there."

"And Tabitha even made friends with their leader, Poseidon!" adds Jesse by hitting Tabitha on the back, who in turn punches him in the stomach.

"Here you are: the Elite students, the future leaders of your Government, and you are buddies with the Rebels who want to destroy your Government," says Tom. "Can you explain the logic to me?"

"We're just silly kids," Jesse replies with an ironic look.

"And yet you still follow the rules set by their so-called 'bad guy' predecessors," Tom tells him.

"No, we're just silly kids, who strangely enough, have resisted indoctrination, and who don't behave like good little sheep," Max answers.

"My mother was a Rebel," says Cathy. "That explains why."

Everyone looks at her with surprise.

An embarrassed silence sets in.

"Right, I'd like to see this famous library," Stephanie tells Tiff.

"Chris, I'm taking you to see our own equipment," says Zayn.

"The rest of you, I'll introduce you to people who will show you parts of the Valley that interest you," says Michelle. "Tabitha, I'm taking you with me."

SOMEWHERE IN CALIFORNIA, 2025, MATT

------------ *Adrien, "underground", 2027*
------------ *Indigo, Paris, 2025*
------------ *Fadi, Egypt, 2025*
------------ *Bart, Indonesia, 2025*
------------ *Matt, California, 2025*
------------ *Sarah, United States, 2022*
------------ *Anna, Lascaux, France, 2006*

I KNOW YOU'RE DEFINITELY GONE.

In recent years, you used to leave for weeks or even months, but we knew that you would come back. We felt your excitement before you would leave us, even though you never told us what you were doing. You always put your lovely finger in front of my mouth when I asked you questions or whenever I wanted to talk to you about my desires to leave too.

Of course, we shared our concerns about the world and where it was heading. Years of economic and political protectionism; countries falling one by one under the spell of charlatans selling them the populist snake oil that fueled the rise of extremism; international non-cooperation resulting in more and more wars powered by religious delusions to cover the real issues; the scramble for dwindling resources, which were increasingly reduced in the face of exponential population growth; the frenzied desire for ever-more consumer goods, driven by multinationals eager for ever-greater profit. A profit that continues to widen the gap between the rich and the poor, with the rich ostentatiously displaying their wealth, and breeding envy and discontent, largely relayed by technology and social networks.

You would tell me that it is easy for me to criticize all this, I who created the social networks and now live with you, my beautiful wife, and our two children, in our beautiful home in Palo Alto. But we have worked together and invested billions to find solutions, first in the fields of health and education, and then against the destruction of our dear planet and all its wonderful and endangered species, and to save us humans, who are busy destroying everything after having taken control of the planet in just a few short millennia.

When you came back from your mysterious travels, I felt a deep sadness in your heart. And then you quickly became the most loving mother and the most wonderful woman again.

This time when you left, you were so sad.

But I have to take care of our children, so we too will hide, with Jeff and the others.

If you ever come back, you will find us, won't you?

We love you so much.

CHAPTER 16

DISCOVERING THE VALLEY

Day 6 of the trip continued, year 2125

MICHELLE TAKES TABITHA WITH her to the lower floors of the Valley. Tabitha follows her with a touch of apprehension. Michelle walks with a decided step and the confidence of a true leader. With her looks, her elegant demeanor, her deep bronze complexion, and her large expressive eyes, she reminds Tabitha of her mother.

"You look a lot like your mother," Michelle says to her without looking back.

"I was thinking exactly the same thing about you, that you also look a lot like her," Tabitha replies.

"It's true that we both got along well."

"Oh, really?"

"Yes, we were very young, like you today, but we shared a lot together in such a short time."

"Like a common passion for education and the common good?"

"Yes, that's exactly what it is," Michelle says, turning to her.

"I listened to many of your conversations during the Valley tour. I must admit that I was really impressed by your level of education."

"Our Founders have invested a lot to ensure that a significant amount of time is spent learning and developing."

"That is also what my mother advocates to the Government."

Tabitha takes her time before continuing.

"Yet the Red World has invested much more in Security and the Army recently. It's the Rebels' fault, as they say."

"Hm, a déjà vu in human history. But that doesn't surprise me, considering some of the people who were with her. I guess it hasn't improved."

Tabitha doesn't answer right away, wondering how much of the Red World's problems to reveal. Several young women of her age come to meet them, offering her the opportunity to stop the conversation.

"This is Tabitha. Take good care of her until dinner at 7:00 p.m. In the main room, of course."

Michelle immediately goes back in the opposite direction.

Stephanie and Tiff enter the library together.

"I don't think I'm going to go out again in the next twenty-four hours," says Stephanie, who can't contain her excitement anymore. "Where should I start?" she asks Tiff.

"There you will find the section on Greek philosophers. Over there the philosophers of the Enlightenment such as Montesquieu, Voltaire, Diderot. The English classics—Shakespeare, Jane Austen, J. K. Rowling. The French Zola, Victor Hugo. The Russians Tolstoy, Dostoevsky. The authors of crime books—my favorite are the Scandinavian and Icelandic authors."

"I still have so much to learn. It's going to take me days. It's extraordinary."

Stephanie suddenly stops.

"What about your history books, art books? I don't see any," she says after having already scanned the different sections.

"We still have a few books of art, especially painting. They are behind this section. History and geography books were systematically suppressed by the Elites. I wasn't there, of course, but apparently some of them came armed, put their sights on everyone, and took away the books that they said were forbidden."

"Do you know what they did with them?"

"I guess they burned them or threw them into the sea. Or are they at your place?"

"I've never seen them before, I can tell you that. Did your predecessors take any notes?"

Stephanie feels Tiff's hesitation.

"You can trust me. I'm not like the ones from twenty-five years ago, I swear."

"Come on, I'll show you."

Tiff takes her to a shelf on which notebooks are placed, appearing absolutely unremarkable to the untrained eye. Stephanie takes one and feels all eyes even more focused on her.

"It's remarkably well-written. Some of you have an eidetic memory, don't you?"

"Not completely. Let's say we have methods, inherited from our ancestors, to improve our memory. Through the generations, we have continued to improve these capacities. One of our ancestors, his name was Elon, had a perfect photographic memory.

Tiff watches Stephanie turn the pages one after the other.

"You, on the other hand, do have it, don't you?"

"Yes, I have absolute memory. It's very convenient, but it can be a heavy burden. Our species has historically been rather murderous and cruel."

"How about I take you to read love stories instead?"

The two new friends look at each other with smiles on their faces.

As he enters the Valley, Max immediately asks what is available in terms of music. Two young people of the same age take him to an entertainment room.

"We stay in touch by telepathy," Tabitha tells them.

"Be careful anyway," adds Leah.

"Don't worry," Chris replies.

He leaves with Zayn to see the "gear" and the control room.

Leah goes to inspect the hospital room and the drug supplies. James goes with the divers to discover the underground mechanisms. Several young women come to pick Tabitha up to show her their underground farming system, based on renewable energy and recycled water.

Cathy and Jesse stay in a corner and look at each other with a complicit look. Both want to see the same thing but are wondering how to formulate it without causing panic in the Valley. Finally, it is Tom, who stands in front of them, fists on his hips, and launches the hostilities:

"Hey, you two! I know where you want to go."

"Can you read minds?" Jesse says to him.

"Let's just say you're pretty easy to read. You want to see our weapons, don't you?"

"Well, since you're offering," he replies nonchalantly, pretending to get up.

"Hey, I didn't say I agreed to take you there!"

"We're going to ask someone else," says Cathy.

"No way. You can only go with me."

"Are you the warden or something?" asks Jesse, laughing.

"No, I'm the only one here who has a chance of controlling you."

Then he goes to an elevator.

"I think you're dreaming, buddy," Jesse says to him. "But nice of you to come with us!"

The elevator goes down to a lower level and Tom takes them to a room where they submit to a fingerprint and a retina reader.

"From now on, an alarm will sound in the control room, and we will be recorded live. Don't talk nonsense!"

"Chris must be up there," says Jesse. "Hi, Chris! You know you have smelly feet, right?"

"What about yours, then!" They hear from some speakers in the weapons room.

"Here's what we have. It's not much, is it?" says Tom to Jesse and Cathy.

Cathy and Jesse are looking everywhere. The equipment is quite varied, with rifles, handguns, knives, bulletproof vests, some drones, and even missile launchers.

"That would make it possible to survive a siege, right?" Cathy asks him.

"Not for long. But above all, these weapons are old. Compared to what you and the others have, we're still a little light, Am I right?"

"We'll take a look at it with Jesse. With some stuff, we have in the shuttle, we may be able to improve the arsenal."

"We're not going to part with our weapons, Cathy," Jesse tells her telepathically.

"It's all right! We have plenty and we will only be gone for ten days, remember. In addition, on some of them, it's just a matter of making some improvements, and it will help them a lot," Cathy answers.

"It's true that they're antiques!"

Tom looks at them as if he could read what they are saying to each other.

But it's not possible. He can't hear us, Cathy thinks to herself.

The afternoon ends with the ringing of a bell calling on the community to go to the relaxation areas. Some will go swimming, others will meet for a drink while listening to music, while still others will put themselves in an armchair to read a book while listening to the ocean.

The cafeteria is also open. The Eight Elites all go there directly, curious to see what those in the Valley are eating.

"The food is mainly based on vegetables, fruit, and fish," Zayn, who came with Chris, tells them.

"Yes, I saw their food production system," says Tabitha. "Everything looks delicious."

"James, you leave us some fish, okay?" says Leah to James, laughing.

"Are you kidding me? There's no way I'm eating my friends!" he says with a wink.

The good mood of the Valley inhabitants is contagious and the Elites allow themselves, for once, to be young among so many others, enjoying the moment. After lunch, Max starts DJ'ing and jumping like a kid with a new toy. The atmosphere around them has relaxed and they are quickly integrated into the different games.

"Cathy, I think he's looking at you," Tabitha says in her ear.

"Who are you talking about?"

"Come on, stop it. You think I haven't seen your little game?"

Tabitha walks away while Cathy can't help but glance at Tom from the corner of her eye. He seems to be in deep conversation with a group. She turns around and immediately feels his gaze on her back.

After a most pleasant evening, the Eight Elites return to sleep in the shuttle. As a precaution, they take turns doing watch. They have taken the stories of Michelle and the helicopters very seriously.

Day 7 of the trip, year 2125

In the morning, after a good night's sleep, they are ready to go again.

"Who wants to eat breakfast here and who prefers to have it in the Valley?" asks Max.

"Very funny!" Tabitha says to him. "Like anyone would prefer our disgusting food."

"Whoa! The first criticism of the Red World I hear from you."

Tabitha shrugs her shoulders and continues to get ready. She takes with her a notebook where she intends to write down everything she learns about agricultural techniques but also everything that the Valley people have learned about the evolution of food over the past one hundred years.

"I will finish this morning what I want to learn and transfer some of my knowledge to them. And you?"

"Same for Cathy and me," Jesse says to her. "We have some adjustments to make to improve their gear and then we're good."

"So, we're leaving after lunch, okay?"

"Oh no, Tab!" Max intervenes. "We still have time. And I could still enjoy a little bit of the Valley. I haven't even gone to see the art books Stephanie tells me about, have I, Steph?"

"Yes, and I too am far from finished reading what I wanted to read," she says.

"I agree to stay," Cathy says. "I promise, we'll leave first thing in the morning. Okay, everyone?"

"All right, all right!" grumbles Tabitha. "But first, we're going to have to face that horrible rain outside."

Indeed, a storm is raging. The sky is menacingly gray-black and in the distance, as they run as fast as possible to reach the Valley's entrance gate, they can hear the waves thundering on the beach and rocks. Suddenly, Max stops and starts dancing, his face toward the sky and his arms wide open. His friends, after a few seconds of bewilderment, all began to imitate him. They finally reach the entrance completely soaked. Their laughter echoes in the hallway, before entering the Valley.

After attending to their various activities, they are now at lunch, enjoying their food.

"Shall we relax this afternoon?" Jesse asks.

"Frankly, we should all leave now," says Tabitha. "It's not conscientious of us to stay."

"We've just spent the last ten years in training every day and being conscientious," Jesse answers. "I say we relax!"

"We relax, my friend!" Max replies by giving him a high five.

"We relax in the library, yeah!" exclaims Stephanie.

"I'm coming with you," Leah says to her. "Come on, Tabitha, come with us. There will be books on agriculture and food, that's for sure."

"I'm going too," James adds. "How about you, Cathy?"

At that moment, Tom approaches the group table, as if he had been waiting for this question.

"I'm taking Cathy with me. I'd like to show her a place that's interesting for her," he says, with a mysterious look.

Cathy looks at Tom with surprise. He can feel James behind her looking at them unhappily.

"With great pleasure," she replies.

Cathy and Tom are walking over the Valley. The rain has finally calmed down and the color of the sky is a soft shade of orange with a mix of unreal colors—as unreal as what is happening now.

Cathy watches Tom walk. He is tall and thin, yet there is an incredible strength and at the same time an urgency, as if everything he does has to be done immediately. He turns towards her and his gaze, with its beautiful green eyes, seems to pass into her soul. He runs his fingers through his curly blond hair and Cathy finds herself wishing that it was her hair that his fingers were stroking.

Tom says, "You're wondering where I'm taking you, aren't you?"

"Do you also read minds?"

He starts laughing and for the first time she feels a special warmth surrounding her.

What the hell is happening to me? Concentrate, Cathy, concentrate, she thinks.

"I just wanted to come up to the surface. I explode underground."

"Is it that hard to live underground?"

"We can't complain. Our system is fine. Obviously, we have some basic rules that serve the good of the community. But apart from that, we live in a very free system. Everyone is educated and pretty cool. That is not the problem."

"What is it then?"

He looks at her intensely and then smiles at her. Cathy is already about to faint when he grabs her by the hand and runs with her in a completely different direction. His grip is firm and warm. Cathy is such a well-trained runner that her legs do all the work, allowing her to concentrate on her hand and the hand that holds it. *How can a hand be so strong and so soft at the same time,* she wonders.

They arrive at the top of a hill and Tom finally lets go of her hand. Cathy then has a strange feeling that she is all alone, already missing the feeling of him touching her.

"You see Cathy, the peaks over there in the distance? They're beautiful and steep. As far back as I can remember, I've dreamed of climbing them. Do you see the sky above? I want to be able to fly there. The sea in the distance, I want to go and see what's beyond it."

He turns to her.

"I'm not cut out to live underground," he says.

Cathy takes her time before answering. She savors the fresh air, the wind caressing her cheek, the smell of grass, the sounds of the nearby waves slamming on the rocks.

"We, too, live locked up, but under a Dome. It's the same thing."

"How is your life there exactly?"

"I'll tell you about it later. But first, the last one to get to the cove is a rotten egg!"

She runs away, with a thrilled Tom chasing after her. Cathy runs but it's as if she's flying with this new freedom that gives her wings.

They arrive at the cove at the same time. Their laughter mingles with the sounds of the birds flying over them. In unison, they throw themselves onto the sand, still fresh from the rains of the past days. The contact refreshes them, after their crazy run. Tom moves closer to Cathy and lies next to her. He stares at her, with his beautiful green eyes that seem to be trying to penetrate her soul. Then he takes her hand in his.

"Tell me about life under the Dome."

Cathy looks at her hand, remembers her mother holding it firmly ten years ago and telling her, "It's going to be okay, it's going to be okay". And then it's as if the gates open and the flood of words finally pour out.

They are so absorbed in their conversation and sharing of secrets that they do not notice the sky slowly turning dark and the cold surrounding them. But above all, they do not see the pair of eyes, a few meters away, staring at them from underneath the water.

The rest of the seventh day goes by too quickly for the Elites. Max leads the entertainment in the evening as he did the day before, and it is quite late when they decide to leave and say goodbye. They all hug each other for a long time and Michelle insists on walking them back to their shuttle.

"Why are you helping us like this, Michelle?" Jesse asks. "What exactly is your real motivation in this?"

"You haven't understood it yet?" replies Michelle.

She looks at them one after the other for a few seconds, then adds:

"Of course, you understood. You can see that our resources are depleting and we will not be able to live like this for much longer. However, we are preparing ourselves, both intellectually and physically. We are preparing to get out of here and to help you when the time comes. For soon this time will come, I see it in you. You will soon be in charge of the Red World. You are our hope, and you will be our salvation."

Then Michelle stares at Jesse, wanting to relay this information to the deepest part of him. "There will be one condition, though, and only one: you will need to bring me Aldo's head."

SOMEWHERE IN CALIFORNIA, 2025, PAOLA

------------ *Adrien, "underground", 2027*
------------ *Indigo, Paris, 2025*
------------ *Fadi, Egypt, 2025*
------------ *Bart, Indonesia, 2025*
------------ *Paola, California, 2025*
------------ *Matt, California, 2025*
------------ *Sarah, United States, 2022*
------------ *Anna, Lascaux, France, 2006*

I KNOW YOU FINALLY LEFT.

They came to warn me and despite the pain of not seeing you for many years, I am so relieved that you went to hide.

Every day without you is tearing me apart. I miss everything. The morning battle to get the kids ready and on time for school, and then the ball in my stomach when I see their two little heads coming into the schoolyard, hoping that no one will hurt them and that everything will go well.

Evening dinners and the four of us discussing the most serious or crazy topics.

Our evenings. Just the two of us in front of Netflix, ashamed to be wasting our time when we have so much to do with the company, our foundations, and other things, but always happy to share a laugh, a disappointment, an emotion together.

Our ski holidays where the afternoons always end with wild snowball fights.

And above all, the evenings when the four of us lie down in the grass to gaze up at and name the stars.

Of course, they're all aware of your plans, with Elon, Jeff, and the others. When they contacted me, all I could think about was protecting you. That was the contract between us: I help them and they'll leave you alone.

I hope one day you will understand that I did all this for you.

They'll leave you alone.

I love you so much.

CHAPTER 17

THE LAST GEOGRAPHICAL COORDINATE

Day 8 of the trip, year 2125

AFTER A SHORT NIGHT, the Elites are now ready. James and Tabitha have started their shuttle, and are trying to reach the last coordinate given by Zeus.

Cathy is still holding in her hand the piece of paper Tom gave her before she left. *Promise you will come back and get me,* he wrote, and she wonders if she will ever be able to keep her promise. But she knows in her heart that she will do everything possible to see him again.

"Maybe we should have left yesterday, like I told you," Tabitha mutters while focusing on the maps Stephanie drew.

With her and Chris' help, Tabitha is trying to find the best way to reach their next destination.

"We are running out of time, that's for sure," says Leah.

"And also, energy to fly the shuttle," James adds. "With this rain yesterday, our batteries couldn't recharge."

"Yes, but it was really worth it," says Stephanie. "What an experience!"

"What did she mean, Michelle, with your father?" asks Cathy innocently to Jesse.

"As if you can't work it out yourself," he says.

"Cathy was too busy with her new friend," adds James.

"Here we are at last," she replies. "You're not going to tell me you're jealous, are you?"

Cathy stands in front of him, her fists clenched on her hips.

"I just wanted to get as much information as I could from him," she says.

"Well, you have a funny way of getting what you want."

Cathy debates with herself between punching him in the face and ignoring him. She chooses the latter option and goes quietly to the back of the shuttle. James turns around, his back arched, and concentrates on the control and navigation screens.

No one dares to move an inch or say a word, not even Jesse, who normally has an easy quip.

It is Tabitha who breaks the silence with a cry of surprise.

"Oh no! Come and see! We are being followed by about a dozen shuttles!"

Everyone rushes to the cockpit to look at the screens. Chris is already typing on his computer to find information.

"They are not from our place, that's for sure," he says.

"Probably the ones Michelle and the others told us about," says Tabitha.

"James, fly as low as possible and go along the coast," suggests Jesse.

"That way, we can always jump in case of an attack," Cathy adds.

"We don't have a chance against them," Max says.

The same heavy silence, as a few minutes ago, has just taken hold. But this time it's for a very different reason.

James finally breaks the silence. "They are always at the same distance."

"Speed up a little to see how they react," Jesse says.

A few tense minutes pass and they can see the points representing the shuttles staying at a similar distance.

"They're not trying to attack us, so maybe we should speed up and try to lose them," suggests Jesse.

"I agree with Jesse, it makes complete sense," adds Stephanie. "They're waiting for us to leave the island."

"Yes, let's go for it," says Cathy.

"All right then, hang on. We'll finally see what this baby is made of," says James, with a touch of excitement in his voice.

All of them buckle themselves in their seats. James waits a few seconds for them all to be secured, then he accelerates like never before.

The aircraft takes a big leap forward, and they can see on the control screens the points representing the other shuttles that are being left behind. They finally disappear. A feeling of relief falls over the group. It is one thing to be confronted with a group of humans in unequal combat and another to be followed by a dozen or so shuttles with at least the same technology as theirs.

"Ugh, who the hell were those guys?" Max asks.

"Guys who didn't want us flying around their neighborhood," Jesse says. "What would we do if a shuttle we didn't know came cruising around near Kantas City?"

"It's so frustrating not knowing how many people we have on Earth," adds Stephanie. "In the end, we don't know any more than those in the Valley."

"And Zeus, who was talking about discovering the truth," Chris wonders aloud. "What exactly is this 'truth?'"

"It's that everywhere in the world there are people with the Mark and with many worlds similar to ours," says Tabitha.

"Did your mother tell you about this before?" asks Cathy.

"As I have already told you, she says that there were other humans who had survived the Ecological Wars," Tabitha replies. "But she never tells me about people with similar technologies."

"But she knew that, didn't she?" asks Cathy.

"Yes, that's right, Cathy," Jesse says. "Aldo and Ariane know about it. Now we know that. But what do we do with this story about the men who had the Mark and saved the islands?"

"And how do you explain why those who live there leave the Valley people alone but shoot them like animals as soon as they try to get out?" adds Max.

"No, they didn't explain that," agrees Cathy. "It's strange."

"And why, when Elite students are sent to the Valley every twenty-five years, this time the Government did not include it in the navigation chart?" asks Jesse.

"Why didn't the current Government act like the previous ones, and why did we get the coordinates from Zeus and not from the Government?" asks Cathy.

"Let's wait and see what we find out at the last coordinates," says Stephanie. "According to what I found in the Valley Library, it should be in a region called Southeast Asia."

"At this rate, we should get there pretty quickly," adds James.

"Good," Jesse says. "Unless we want to be island warriors for the rest of our lives, we don't have time to hang around."

"If we ever do come back to Kantas City," remarks Max.

Everyone looks at him and wonders if he's serious or if it's another one of his jokes.

"What, don't look at me like that! James, don't you see yourself splashing around in the water and spending all day with your fish buddies?"

"And what about our responsibilities, what do you do with them?" asks Leah. "There's the small matter of 100,000 people to govern in Kantas City, for example."

"Precisely," says Max. "Am I really the only one who would spend my life in the Valley, in a dream setting, surrounded by intelligent, educated, fun and sensible people? Who wants to return to a society where everyone goes about their work without questioning it? In a society where those who do not follow the rules lose their jobs and their families? A society guarded by an army of psychopaths?"

"Honestly, Max, you think we could just drop everything and go live there, without any reaction from the Government?" asks Tabitha, annoyed. "After all they've invested in our training?"

"And all this to become fugitives and have to hide all the time," adds Stephanie.

"But on top of all the reasons you mention, we have such an important role to play, a crucial role for the future of the Red World and its inhabitants," says Cathy. She stands in front of Max with her arms crossed, feeling more determined than she ever had before.

"Oh my God, girls, let's calm down," Max answers, covering his face. "I was just saying you can dream sometimes, can't you? You girls are so serious," he adds, exhaling.

Jesse, Chris, and James can't stop laughing

But Max is quietly thinking to himself, *Someday. Someday.*

The rest of the trip goes smoothly, without any further source of tension, without any shuttles in sight. They take the opportunity to share what they have learned during the two days in the Valley. They are constantly amazed at the community's operating model, the knowledge of the group members and the ingenuity of the Founders. But they also discuss the limitations of this model and its application for a larger group, as well as the resources that will soon be lacking in the Valley.

Cathy recounts all the talks she had on the beach with Tom, his aspiration to discover the world and his frustration at being trapped underground. Yet she chooses to keep to herself the note he wrote to her and her silent promise, as well as what she feels for him. But the others are not fooled; they who know her so well, especially Leah and James, exchange worried glances.

A few hours later, they approach their destination. They have flown over land for several minutes where nothing but thick forests were visible and without any signs of human activity. Now the sea surrounds them and the water is clearer than anything they have seen before. It's as if the madness of men had failed to reach this part of the world. And this is confirmed when they approach the coordinates given by Zeus.

"It's a joke," Max laughs.

"Did your friend Zeus decide to show us the most beautiful thing on earth?" Stephanie asks Chris.

Ahead of them lies an island with beaches that run for several kilometers. James and Tabitha, at the controls as always, decide to fly over it.

"The island must have about fifty kilometers of coastline," Tabitha tells them. "And the hill you see there must be about 650 meters high."

"It's amazing how dense this jungle is," adds Cathy.

"And what beaches!" exclaims Max. "All different and all beautiful."

"Well, shall we go down?" asks Leah. "We have to explore."

"Do you feel any presence, girls?" Jesse asks Tabitha and Cathy.

"No!" they say in chorus.

"However, there were humans who lived there," says Stephanie. "Look at this peninsula and the remains of the statue. It looks strangely similar to the one we saw on the first island."

"And some of them came not long ago," James adds. "Look, there's a perfect airstrip ahead of us."

"It has not quite been a year since the trees were cut," Max continues. "Shuttles like ours have also come here."

"We're going down," James replies.

The landing is a little rough and everyone puts on their equipment and weapons before leaving. The shuttles that followed them earlier in the day have increased their vigilance. Not knowing what technology they are dealing with, they prefer not to rely solely on Tabitha's and Cathy's gifts.

When they come out, a damp heat hits them in the face.

"I don't think our suits will protect us," Jesse says, jokingly. "Wouldn't we be better off naked?"

"Completely naked with your dagger, I would like to see that," Cathy adds with a laugh.

"I would look great, there's no doubt about it."

While joking, the Eight are exploring the area, with their senses on alert, staying at a respectable distance from their shuttle. Chris and Stephanie have computers in their hands while the other six record information with their long-distance cameras.

"There's something written there, near the beach," Cathy says.

They all run after her.

"Welcome to Koh Samui, the most beautiful beaches in the world, the Full Moon Party and Thai boxing," reads Cathy, on a beachside sign that has recently been put up again.

"Is this some kind of joke?" asks Stephanie.

"Wow, it looks like fun here," says Max. "Full Moon Party!"

"Especially Thai boxing," Jesse adds. "My dream! My dream!"

"Thai boxing, or muay-thai, is a martial art of the foot and fist boxing genre, which originates in the traditional practices of Krabi-krabong and Muay Boran," recites Stephanie.

"Wow, my favorite martial art," Jesse says.

"Sorry, folks," James says as he undresses, "but the sea is calling me."

"Are you going to try to find something or are you just going to get wet?" asks Jesse with a smile.

"I'm going to ask the fish if they saw anything. Max, will you come with me?"

"I don't technically speak fish unless you find a dolphin. If they still exist," he adds with a sad look. "Humans are really a very stupid species. The dolphins seemed so beautiful and intelligent."

"Come on, Max, think of the Full Moon Party," Jesse tells him, patting him on the shoulder.

"Come and see over there, there are traces of a camp," says Stephanie, looking at her screen.

They let James dive into the clearest water they've ever seen.

"Say hello to the fish from us," jokes Max.

He watches James with envy, like all the others. James dives and dives again, making no attempt to hide his pleasure. His friends then see him swimming at an incredible speed on the other side of the beach. He will complete the tour of the island in no time. Meanwhile, the rest of the troop ventures a little further into the jungle.

Chris and Leah decide to patrol close to the shuttle.

"What do you think of Cathy falling in love with this Tom?" asks Leah

"What are you talking about?"

"Are you telling me you didn't notice?"

"Well, no."

"You're hopeless. It's as obvious as the nose on your face. I am worried about it."

"You shouldn't worry about it. It's Cathy. She will always put our group's interests ahead of her own.

"That's what worries me."

The other five walk behind Stephanie, who has her nose glued to her screen. Finally, after about ten minutes, they find themselves in a camp. This one is perfectly hidden in the jungle and would have been impossible to find without their equipment.

"Bingo," Jesse says. "Well done, Steph. You're a star."

"It's far from the comfort of the Valley, just a makeshift hut," notes Max.

"Yes, but made with products from before the Ecological Wars," adds Stephanie, pointing at goods that certainly do not come from nature.

"And it's extremely well organized and well hidden," says Cathy.

"The people who used to live here hide and they know how to hide well," Jesse adds.

"Anything interesting to take?" Cathy asks.

"Yes, I found a book," says Stephanie. "I'm taking it with me."

"Okay, we'll quickly go back to the beach. Hope James will have found something," Cathy says.

They leave as quickly as possible, taking great care not to leave any trace of their visit. When they arrive on the beach, James is emerging from the water. The others can see on his face that he has some good news to share. They are joined by Leah and Chris.

"So, did you find any dolphins?" Max asks him.

"Even better. There are boats hidden all around the island, some in caves accessible only from the sea."

"The people living here have thought of everything. Probably so they can escape in the event of an attack," says James. "It seems they have the same friends as the ones in the Valley, don't they, Chris?"

"Indeed. Those who landed on this island have very advanced technology."

"Much more advanced than what we saw in the camp over there, no doubt," adds Stephanie.

"I don't think there's anyone human here except us," Tabitha says, "but I'd like to check again."

"Okay, but no more than thirty minutes to explore," Chris tells them. "I have a bad feeling about this after what we saw when we left the Valley, and I think we're far too exposed here."

"I'll stay with you," Stephanie suggests.

"Me too," says Leah. "Cathy, Jesse, Tabitha, and Max are much better runners than I am."

"There are a lot of animals around and they are not starving," says Max. "It is better if I stay with you, you never know."

"I'm going back into the water," says James.

"We take our radios," says Cathy. "Do we do teams of two? Max, will you come with me?"

"So easy," Tabitha says, giving her a pat on the back. "You take the one who talks to animals!"

"And you are the best guy ever, aren't you, Jesse?" asks Cathy.

"Absolutely Cathy," he replies. "Come on, let's go for it. Ciao, folks!"

The four of them start running towards the jungle.

Chris watches them leave with apprehension.

"Girls, we're going to go to our shuttle. I'd like to get it off the ground and turn on all the radars. I'm telling you, I have a bad feeling about this place. I hope for our sake that I'm not discovering a new gift for myself."

Leah and Stephanie nod and leave after him.

Meanwhile, Cathy and Tabitha continue to joke together through the radio. Each couple heads in a different direction.

"You're going to get eaten first, Cathy, that's for sure," Tabitha teases her. "Max can't talk to spiders and I just met some huge ones."

"Ha ha, not even afraid," she says laughing.

"I know you don't like spiders and there are some impressive ones here. There are also scorpions and giant snakes."

"They are just little creatures."

"Too bad they didn't put snakes in our training room. We're out of practice!"

"Did you hear that noise, Tab?" asks Max over the radio.

Tabitha suddenly stops.

"Chris, Leah, and Steph have just taken off in our shuttle."

Indeed, they see the aircraft passing over them, towards the other side of the island.

"What do we do now? Should we follow them?" asks Max.

"Wait, no more noise. I hear shuttles coming in our direction. In fact, I hear two," Tabitha tells them.

"Let's have a look," exclaim Jesse and Cathy at the same time.

The four run as fast as they can through the hostile jungle to reach the airstrip. When they arrive at the edge of the forest, they can see two small fighter planes, which landed in the same place as their shuttle a few minutes ago.

"Jesse, they look like replicas of the MiG-21," Cathy says to him.

"Ah yes, the famous Mikoyan-Gurevich 21, adored by the Russians before the wars," he replies.

"These ones are two-seater planes. I see two men near the beach and two near the planes," says Cathy.

"Do you hear what they're saying?" Jesse asks Tabitha.

"No, they aren't talking," she replies. "But from their clothes and the way they move, I would say they are very well-trained soldiers."

"And they are also too far away for me to understand their intentions," adds Cathy. "I need to get closer."

"If they're here to shoot us, we're going to have to get them now, because when they're in the air, it's going to be more difficult," Jesse adds.

"Shall we both go over to them, Jesse?" Cathy asks.

"Okay. Max and I will stay on the edge of the jungle to cover you," Tabitha says.

The four friends move very fast, making as little noise as possible, and staying hidden in the jungle. Cathy and Jesse emerge and move forward with their hands held forward, as a sign of peace. The other men immediately turn towards them with raised weapons.

"We just want to talk to you," Jesse shouts.

All around them, life has stopped.

There is no longer a sound coming from the jungle. All the birds have halted their songs, as if they too are listening to the drama that is about to unfold.

Only the slight sound of the waves can be heard in the distance. The sea is impassive in the face of man's violence.

Max, Tabitha, Jesse, and Cathy all have their senses on alert to anticipate each movement of the four men in front of them.

Finally, one of them gives a signal. They all start shooting. Jesse and Cathy throw themselves on the ground to avoid the bullets. Tabitha and Max are shooting to cover them. With great difficulty, Jesse and Cathy manage to return to the jungle.

"Are you guys okay?" asks Max.

"I got hit in the leg," says Jesse. "But I can still walk. We need to stop them before they leave. Let's go out again, this time all four of us. Let's do it like we do in practice, okay?"

They come out of the jungle and run toward the men, moving in an unpredictable manner and firing fast and accurately.

The two men who were by the beach are now running to the fighter planes. One of them pulls out a machine gun, slowing the Elites' progress in their direction.

"They're about to take off!" Cathy shouts through the piercing noises of the bullets whizzing around them.

"They took James' stuff!" adds Tabitha.

"We have to hurry! Come on!" screams Jesse.

Suddenly, one of their attackers puts what looks like a rocket launcher on his shoulder. The Elites try to withdraw as quickly as possible and the first grenade lands near them, blowing everything up around them. They are about to enter the jungle when a second one barely misses them. Meanwhile, the first fighter plane is taking off in their pursuit. It quickly passes over them and then goes back to position itself in front of them.

"Everyone run!" screams Cathy.

The four friends go deeper into the jungle. They use their machetes to tear down all obstacles. The intensive training they received in the Dome is finally serving them and they advance so fast that the last grenade lands a few meters behind them.

"Let's keep going that way," Cathy shouts.

In front of them stands a tall mountain, which they try to circumvent to prevent themselves from being seen.

They hear a third explosion behind them, then a fourth. Their attackers are trying to shoot them but they have not yet been able to follow the movements of the Eight, especially since they are zigzagging.

Just then, their own shuttle passes over the mountain, and with a single shot, blows up the fighter plane that remained on land, as well as the two men beside it. The second plane is splashed as it flies over the sea.

The sky has turned pink as the aircraft's debris disperses into the ocean.

"Well, then! I didn't know they were so good at flying," says Max, really surprised by the skill of his classmates.

"Chris also had to find a way to make the plane undetectable on radar," says Tabitha. "He was working on it with me on our last trip, another type of jammer."

They run back to meet their shuttle that has landed right next to the burning carcass of the fighter jet.

Jesse is limping in pain.

"Ah, it was you, James," Max says to him.

"Yes, they picked me up a little further down the coast. I stayed in the water to observe them until you arrived. Then I went to meet Chris, Steph, and Leah who were positioned behind that mountain."

"You could have arrived a little earlier," says Cathy sulking. "They almost blew us up."

"Don't worry, there is no way they could have killed you," says Stephanie.

"Of course not," Jesse laughs. "Ouch! It hurts!"

“Come on, show me your wound,” whispers Leah, as she starts to inspect the bloody leg. Then she gently lays her hands on the wound.

“I’m not waiting for more planes to arrive. We’re leaving!” James exclaims.

“We have to find out where the people who lived in the camp are,” says Cathy.

“If there are any left,” Tabitha says. “The guys from the two planes weren’t here just for fun and the Full Moon Party. What makes you think those in the camp weren’t killed by them?”

“Her instinct and mine too,” intervenes Chris.

“Yes, because during your absence, Chris became a psychic,” adds Stephanie. “It’s true, I’m not lying to you!”

“So that’s why you left with the shuttle?” Cathy asks him.

“Yes, my friend. I sensed the danger and their arrival. And I bet that those who lived here are over there, on another island, hiding.”

“We’re going to fly over to the surrounding islands, and let Tabitha find them,” James suggests.

“As for me, I found a way to make our shuttle invisible from the radar,” Chris adds. “Well, with the tricks I know. But it worked with these two planes. We’ll see.”

“We’re not going to hang around,” says James, cooled down by the meeting with the two planes.

As they talk, they inspect the debris from the exploded aircraft and burned bodies.

“Well, then, who were those guys?” asks Tabitha.

“I have no idea,” James and Chris reply in unison.

SOMEWHERE IN SINGAPORE, 2024, NAYELI

------------ *Adrien, "underground", 2027*
------------ *Indigo, Paris, 2025*
------------ *Fadi, Egypt, 2025*
------------ *Bart, Indonesia, 2025*
------------ *Paola, California, 2025*
------------ *Matt, California, 2025*
------------ *Nayeli, Singapore, 2024*
------------ *Sarah, United States, 2022*
------------ *Anna, Lascaux, France, 2006*

NAYELI WAKES UP AND massages her temples.

These damned nightmares, always the same. She sees herself walking in the streets of a city where there is no one left. She looks out the windows and sees only corpses, some stacked on top of each other. She starts running and screaming but no one can answer her.

I spent too much time with Greenpeace, it must be because of that, *she tells herself. She has been an activist for the environmental organization for a few years, first in Mexico City, then in Southeast Asia. She had visited the region from top to bottom and witnessed incredible destruction: the destroyed seabed; the decimated forests; the slaughtered animals; the polluted air. While most people her age were only interested in consuming and showing off on social networks, she and her friends preferred to chain themselves to trees or to demonstrate.*

It was exciting, but most of all it made sense.

They often debated, horrified by the greed of corporations, the corruption, the rise of injustice in the world while the masses were blinded by the desire to always have more, cultivated by the media, advertising, and international consumer icons. But each time, they agreed that non-violent activism remained the most effective form and most in line with their values to try to change the world. This small and diverse group of young people from all over the world had formed during various adventures, parties, and struggles, but together they were united. They had decided to study, taking an MBA program in Management of International Organizations and NGOs in Singapore, in order to acquire as many skills as possible for the success of their common project.

Nayeli touches her shoulder unconsciously, as she has often done recently. They all know each other, but she hasn't talked about the Mark yet. Every time she thinks about talking about it, she sees her grandmother screaming: "Never show it, Nayeli, never show it, or they will burn you alive!"

Her grandmother had been the idol of her childhood. She was a colorful character who had borne Nayeli's mother late in life. "I was having too much fun before," she would say to her. She, who had practically raised her and taught her never to doubt herself and to make the world her playground. She remembered as if it was yesterday the day she introduced her to reading the tarot, saying with a big wink, "You are a witch like me, so it's time you learn."

When the Mark had first appeared, Nayeli was staying with her grandmother in Mexico, which had happened too rarely in recent years. She had naturally shown her shoulder. Her grandmother had started screaming, swearing, blessing herself, calling all the gods and demons in the world. Nayeli looked at her, terrified. When she finally calmed down, the grandmother told her that the whole family's line of women came from a small village in the mountains of northern Catalonia, before they emigrated to Mexico. A long time ago, women also had this Mark on their left shoulder blade. And then men of the Church, with large black coats and huge crosses, had come to burn them, at least those who had not been able to hide.

Her grandmother was sure of it. She had even shown her drawings, transmitted from mother to daughter. It was exactly the same Mark.

CHAPTER 18

SEARCHING FOR SURVIVORS

Day 8 of the trip continued, year 2125

THEY LEAVE THE ISLAND called Koh Samui at full speed. They are back in the shuttle and are quickly cleaning themselves. Jesse's leg is already perfectly healed, thanks to Leah's attentive care and exceptional gift.

Stephanie is absorbed by the book she found in the camp.

"What are you doing, Stephanie?" asks Jesse. "Did you find a book on anatomy?"

"You can be so thick sometimes! You really are from Dauntless, that's for sure."

"What are you talking about?"

"And you, Leah, are from Abnegation, and Max is from Amity. I'm from Erudite, of course, like Chris. Cathy is from Candor."

Everyone is wondering what is going through her mind, and in answer to their puzzled looks, Stephanie relates a summary of the book.

"Of course, it's a work of fiction," she adds. "The author imagined a possible future, which could have been ours."

"Isn't our organization in Kantas City the same?" asks Max. "The Actives grouped by Centers, and therefore by capacities and strengths, determined at the end of the first cycle of Compulsory Education?"

"That is the very principle of an organized society," says Tabitha. "Chaos doesn't work. Not for a large society."

"As for us, we are future Divergents," says Cathy.

"But each of us is chosen to join a different Unit," replies Tabitha. "You – Justice; Max – Arts and Nature; Jesse – Strategy; Chris – Science; Leah – Medicine; Stephanie – Education; me – Administration; and James – Army. Even if I still have my doubts about that last one."

Everyone laughs except James, who looks falsely offended.

"You must admit that I am an excellent pilot," he adds. "It's already a start."

They continue to laugh. The idea of James replacing Aldo, Jesse's father, seems so absurd to them.

"We may be Divergents in the sense that we, too, are rebelling against the established order," Max adds.

"And why do you think we are being sent to the rest of the world for ten days?" retorts Tabitha, clearly annoyed.

"So that we can fit nicely into the mold when we get back," Jesse says with a cynical look.

"We'll see if we fit into the mold, we'll see," Cathy says thoughtfully.

That concludes the discussion.

They have already flown over several scattered islands, passing them as close as possible, when Tabitha cries out victoriously.

"There! I think we found them. I'm pretty sure I heard voices!"

"All right, let me find a place to land," James says.

The island is quite small, no more than two kilometers square. They fly over the few mountains to find the right terrain when they come across a lagoon. It has the appearance of an old volcanic crater, with beaches around it, and above all hidden from view and surrounded by a lush forest.

"The place is magical," exclaims Leah.

"And we're going to make it even more magical by hiding our shuttle," Chris adds.

James gently lands the shuttle on the beach and moves into the jungle. The group of friends leaves the shuttle and start covering it with everything they can find: foliage, tree trunks, bark. The entire team works assiduously and eventually their shuttle becomes hidden. Tabitha pauses from time to time to listen to the sounds around the island.

They finish equipping themselves to go exploring when Max warns them to be quiet.

"Even though the island is small, there are lots of animals on it. It's going to be interesting."

"It's not just animals," Tabitha says excitedly, "I can hear five people coming in our direction."

"Probably to watch us," Jesse adds. "How about a little hunt?"

"But we don't shoot anyone, okay?" states Leah, staring at Jesse with a serious and determined look.

"Why do you think I always want to kill everyone?" he replies, annoyed. "Say it to Cathy instead. She has an excellent record."

"Both of you stop," says Tabitha. "Does everyone have their own radio? And are you ready for the hunt?"

Everyone nods. They don suits, helmets, infrared sight masks, various daggers, and pistols—an elite commando unit. Jesse takes command during the expedition.

A palpable excitement grips the group, due as much to the prospect of meeting new people as to the hunt in the jungle.

"Still five people, Tabitha?" asks Jesse.

"Yes. They're not far away. We could almost wait for them here."

"That would be too easy. No way we will spoil the fun. Let's go!"

The friends move into the jungle. Soon, they begin to spread out to surround their targets. The best runners, James, Cathy, Max, and Tabitha, go in front. When they arrive near the five targets, they move around making noise to drive their quarry toward the center. Tabitha provides live updates by radio and Jesse gives the orders. They have trained many times in these urban guerrilla techniques, often in the Obama district, just for fun. But it is nothing like what they are facing now: the jungle, with its natural obstacles, smells and humidity, the sounds of birds and animals, and the blue sky contrasting with the green and brown mass around them. The pleasure they experience almost makes them forget that they are about to meet other humans, with their own story that may shed light on their own. Jesse coordinates the orchestra, signaling them to take turns making noise, to better attract their prey into their nets. Gradually, the trap is closing.

"Don't come closer than fifteen meters," Jesse whispers to them. "Wait for my signal."

When the circle is perfectly formed around the five targets, Jesse gives the signal to approach the small group. They discover two women in their forties and three teenagers.

The first woman is tall, thin, and very muscular. She has very short blond hair and piercing blue eyes. It is she who holds a rifle, which appears to be very modern, contrasting with the simplicity of her worn and patched clothing. The other woman is incredibly beautiful. She is smaller but her features, highlighted by her pale brown skin, are breathtaking. The three teenagers, two boys and a girl, are all of average height. They have slightly dark skin, black eyes, bold and intelligent looks. They look at the commando of the Eight, fearless, firmly holding their daggers and makeshift clubs.

Tabitha hears the tall blond woman say in a low voice to the woman next to her, "All these battles, all these sacrifices, just to end like this."

"We didn't come to kill you," Tabitha tells them. "Well, actually, Cathy, what do you think?"

"Absolutely not psychopaths, that's for sure," she replies. "On the contrary, they're fantastic!"

Chris can't contain his excitement when he adds:

"I feel that this will be very interesting for us. We can trust them."

And on that note, the Eight begin to take off their masks.

The five people in front of them cannot hide their surprise.

"But you are kids," exclaims the tall blonde, who seems to be the leader of the group.

"Yes, but very resourceful kids," Jesse replies, laughing.

"Where are you from? We saw your shuttle arrive. This is the first time we've seen one like it. Although we've seen a lot of others," she adds.

"We have come a long way," says Cathy, who is immediately attracted by the woman's charisma. *She reminds me so much of my mother,* she thinks.

"You really shouldn't be afraid of us," adds Chris, who sees the gray color of fear around them and tries to reassure them. "It's a long story, we'll tell you about it later. But know that we've come in peace. We were actually given the geographical coordinates of Koh Samui, not here."

"Have you found one of our campsites?" asks the other woman with the pale brown skin.

"Absolutely," Jesse answers. "And we even took the opportunity to blow up two fighter planes and four people, who, with all due respect, didn't seem to be coming out of the jungle like you."

"Are you kidding me? You just put us all in great danger!"

"Oh no, it's great, well done!" one of the young people tells them, smiling. "If they could have, they would have blown you up."

"Yes, we noticed," Max says with a smile. "I think we can all put our weapons down, can't we? My name is Max," he says, approaching the teenager, who shakes his hand and is also smiling.

They all introduce themselves. The three young people do not hide their excitement at meeting them. After agreeing to go back to their camp, they bombard them with questions. Max, Leah,

Chris, and Stephanie answer them with pleasure and often with a lot of fun. Chris sees many positive colors around the teenagers and immediately feels a desire to protect them.

Jesse and Tabitha are walking a little behind. They do not feel as comfortable as the others to so quickly share their knowledge with complete strangers.

"In two days, we will be back in Kantas City and we will start our training in the respective units. And now we're walking with people who live on tropical islands. What do you think about all this?" Tabitha asks Jesse.

"I think we are opening our eyes to the reality of the world outside Kantas City, as well as what's going on inside, good and bad."

"Yes, the good as well as the bad. What about us, the Eight, in all this? We have shown differences of opinion, haven't we?"

"I didn't tell you this before, but before we left my father recommended that I stay close to you during the journey. I think that they really were at each other's throats during their ten-day outing twenty-five years ago. I think we're doing okay. We have gotten along pretty well."

"I didn't know Aldo held me in such high esteem. Considering he and my mother hate each other so much. Do you think we've all changed in just a few days?"

"Have your opinions changed?" Jesse asks her.

"No, not that much. I mean, I don't know, maybe. The others in front, however... I'm afraid Cathy will react strangely tomorrow when we get back to Toledo."

Jesse glances at her.

"You know, Poseidon is nice to look at."

Tabitha punches him in the shoulder, which makes Jesse laugh a lot.

James, Cathy, and the two women turn around to watch Jesse and Tabitha bickering.

Cathy is trying to probe the mind of the tall blond girl whose name is Ellen.

"You look at me a lot. You're Cathy, right?"

"It hasn't always been easy to live in the jungle, has it?"

"I don't know anything different. What's hard is to lose the people you love, without really understanding why."

The other woman, called Ann, takes her hand and looks at her with great kindness.

Homosexuality is completely accepted in Kantas City, but she has never before seen such love reveal itself so clearly in the eyes of two women.

"Have you ever left this archipelago?" asks James, who is joining the conversation.

"These islands are our territory. There are many of them and we go from island to island where we have camps. But yes, some of us have left."

"Go on," says Jesse, who has approached the group with Tabitha.

"There are many small camps scattered like ours, from descendants of survivors. But there are also more advanced societies. They're far away, inland. You met some earlier, didn't you? And I'm sure that they came out of hiding in a cave, like our people did, a long time ago."

"A cave? Like the white man on the first island!" exclaims James.

"We're here!" one of the teenagers shouts to them.

A group of children begin to run towards them. They are not afraid of the Elites, as if it was completely natural to see eight young people arriving in very sophisticated clothes in complete contrast to what they are wearing. Chris and his friends are surprised at first, but let themselves be won over by the children's high spirits.

"We'll figure out this cave story later," says Chris with a wide smile because he sees only warm and positive colors around the people.

Everything here is different from the Valley or the first villages visited. There is a set of shelters, slightly elevated to protect against insects, parasites, and reptiles, but otherwise completely integrated into nature. Anyone flying over the area could not see the village. Inside the shelters, rudimentary tools and utensils are mixed with products from advanced societies. Chris notices a few computers, radios, and transmitters.

The whole group of about forty people come together to give them a warm welcome.

Cathy looks toward her friends with a complicit smile.

Ellen gathers everyone in a more open place, with a kind of stove buried in the ground. It is surely the place where they eat and where they gather together. Ellen is undoubtedly their leader. Everyone shows her great respect. Cathy continues to scrutinize her with a touch of admiration. *She reminds me so much of my mother,* she says to herself again.

Ellen quickly introduces them to the Eight. Everyone looks at them with great interest.

A young boy no older than eight years old, unable to stay still and running around the group, asks the first question:

"They say you shot down planes. Is that true? Is that true?"

The whole group starts laughing and Chris takes the floor.

"We had come to see the island but they attacked us, so we had no choice. We didn't want to kill them."

Chris resembles many of them and it is clear that his words, in addition to his personal aura, make a great impression on the group.

"So, tell us how you escaped," asks another boy.

The Eight Elites look at each other, curiously.

Chris answers them: "Escaped? But where do you think we escaped from?"

Ellen then intervenes in the conversation:

"From one of the cities where the planes came from. From these cities, one can only want to escape.

"There's been a misunderstanding," says Chris. "We come from cities, but they are very far from here, hours and hours away in our shuttle."

"Have you seen these cities?" Cathy cuts in, unable to contain her curiosity.

"None of us here, but we have heard stories from travelers passing through. As you can see, bartering for what they bring from these cities can be very important to us," she says, pointing to her pistol.

"And why would anyone want to escape from it?"

The group starts laughing.

Ellen begins her story.

"From what we know, and all the stories match, cities are very special and dangerous places. It seems that everything there is very clean and orderly. The technology is very advanced. Unfortunately, the notion of freedom has been eliminated. Everything is regulated, from birth to death, and those who rebel are killed. There are dictators with powerful armies. It is very difficult to escape, but some succeed and join us in the jungle. It's true that we don't have much comfort, but we hunt and gather, and we love each other," she says with a smile.

"Can you believe it? They don't even give them names there. Only numbers!" says one of the teenagers who accompanied them earlier.

"So, if you haven't escaped, what are you doing here?" Ellen asks Cathy, with a hint of suspicion in her voice.

"We've come a long way, as Chris told you," she says. "We left to see the world as it's part of our training. We received the coordinates of Koh Samui as a place where we would meet other groups that had survived the Ecological Wars. Our city is called Kantas City, and it is the main city of the Red World."

"Well," exclaims Ellen. "Here, cities are part of the Yellow World."

The Eight all look at each other with amazement.

"Look at that! That's even more interesting," Jesse says, pointing to Ellen.

She has just taken off the long-sleeved T-shirt she was wearing, and he can now see her bare left shoulder. Embedded in the skin, like a tattoo, is The Mark.

SOMEWHERE IN KOH SAMUI, YEAR 2026

------------ *Adrien, "underground", 2027*
------------ *Nayeli, Koh Samui, 2026*
------------ *Indigo, Paris, 2025*
------------ *Fadi, Egypt, 2025*
------------ *Bart, Indonesia, 2025*
------------ *Paola, California, 2025*
------------ *Matt, California, 2025*
------------ *Nayeli, Singapore, 2024*
------------ *Sarah, United States, 2022*
------------ *Anna, Lascaux, France, 2006*

NAYELI AND HER FRIENDS decide to celebrate the first anniversary of their lives in the caves. They raise their glasses and toast "the end of the world." This immediately provokes crying, laughter and a lot of hugging. They are, of course, all thinking of their families and friends who may or may not be somewhere in the world. There is no longer any means of communication. For them, coming from a generation where most people spent more time on their smartphones than talking to other human beings, it is a big change.

Nayeli had had nightmares for months, and then one night she woke up with the conviction that she would have to hide. In fact, in her dream, she saw her grandmother telling her to go to the caves. By caves, she meant the ancient underground temples she had visited in Koh Samui a few years ago. Of course, her grandmother had never been to Thailand before, but this detail did not seem particularly important to her. What bothered her was how she was going to convince her group of friends to come with her. She spent a few days thinking about her options and then finally decided to organize a surprise excursion and ask them to trust her. She felt that they had to be there in exactly twenty-eight days. Her friends, always ready for adventure and under the pressure of her pleas, accepted.

She had left, alone, a week before, and spent her time discreetly storing in the caves everything she could buy in the supermarkets—the 7-Eleven and the FamilyMart—on the island. It was a lot. She had given a few thousand baht to some local people to protect the site and keep potential tourists away. She had also stored everything she thought was important to have for a long period of time, such as batteries, lamps, matches, hygiene products, medicine, and all the computer equipment she had.

When her friends arrived at Koh Samui airport, she put them all in the back of her rental truck, and took them to their underground temple. She had told them that they would experience living a week underground in a sacred temple. She had hidden most of the supplies under tarps and had shown them only a small part of the place.

The first night had gone well. They were all excited to live this experience. There was no telephone network and they felt as though they were living in the previous millennium. Except that they had good food, board games and books.

The next day, they heard a loud bang. "It must be an earthquake," she told them. Yet she knew deep down that the nightmare she had had many times had become a reality.

Finally, the week passed. Just before they were due to leave, Nayeli told them the story of the Mark, her premonitions, and all the provisions she had prepared for them. They knew Nayeli well enough to know that, as incredible as it might seem, she would never have done any of this for nothing. They agreed to wear the protective masks she had prepared. It was well for them that they did so. Because when they came out, the air was unbreathable, and everything was chaos around them.

CHAPTER 19

RETURN TO TOLEDO

Day 8 of the trip continued, year 2125

THE EVENING WITH ELLEN and her friends is simple and at the same time completely unreal.

The Eight reveal the Mark that they also each have.

Ellen tells them the story of their ancestors, and of the others that are on other islands.

In particular there is the story of Nayeli, who had saved the first group, and who also carried the Mark.

Especially about Nayeli's premonition that led her to save her friends.

Of the first years and their adaptation to the new way of life of hunters and gatherers.

The incessant stalking of Yellow World planes, trying to eliminate them.

Witches from the past that were burned alive long ago, because they too had the Mark.

Leah cannot help but examine everyone, giving them all her recommendations. They share with her the secrets of the plants they know and use, such as *Andrographis paniculata,* anti-inflammatory or anti-diarrhea, or turmeric, to treat skin inflammation and wounds as well as stomach ulcers.

Chris examines their computers and other devices and is unable to resist tinkering with them. Leah, Stephanie, James, and Tabitha return to the shuttle to get medicines and clothes, as well as various products that may be useful to the Islanders—all this under Tabitha's meticulous supervision.

They eat fish, bananas, small pineapples, mango, guava, drink coconut juice, and even try insects and reptiles—a real feast.

They laugh a lot, some telling stories of hunting, fishing, love, and the myths and legends around the Yellow World. The Eight, especially Max and Jesse, who have the gift of turning every drama into a funny story, tell them about their lives, their city, their training, the battles, the members of the Government. Max's imitation of Aldo has a particularly strong impact on the younger ones who hide behind the grown-ups seized with laughter.

Finally, after a long night, the Eight leave to join the shuttle. They decide to leave the island as soon as possible, to avoid attracting the Yellow World planes to their hosts.

They hug each other for a long time, promising to see each other again one day. A short but exceptional encounter. But no one is asking to come with them to Kantas City. They cherish their way of life too much, even if they do recognize the permanent danger they are in. The stories of the Yellow World have definitely jaded them against life in the city. Some have reflected that the Red World, as described by the Eight, sounds too much like the Yellow World.

Ellen hugs Cathy a little tighter than the others. "You look like my mother," Cathy tells her.

"Then you will be my adopted daughter," Ellen replies, deeply touched.

"How about we go see these cities of the Yellow World?" suggests Jesse as the shuttle takes off.

"I don't think it's a good idea," Tabitha replies. "I want to go back to Kantas City safe and sound."

"Are you not curious? We are superheroes! Nothing can hurt us!"

"Stop talking nonsense," Cathy says. "We will have plenty of time, after our return to Kantas City, to come back and explore this part of the world. Then we can discover who those who live in the Yellow World are. The Government is aware of the place, that's for sure."

"And remember, we are invited tonight to Toledo," Max adds.

"It's going to be a long way home," concludes James. "Our batteries are running low."

"Well, then! So much for the brave superheroes," grumbles Jesse before immediately falling asleep.

Day 9 of the trip, year 2125

This conversation is followed by a night and a day in flight.

They return to the same path they had followed on the way here: the same jungles, then the snow-covered mountains, the colorful deserts, and finally "their" desert.

They could have spent the whole day debating the Red World, but they are all looking forward to seeing the familiar colors again.

When they arrive at the Red World, they take the time to stop in several small towns. Each time, much to their astonishment and displeasure, they only arouse fear or even terror.

Finally, the day is already well advanced when they see the outline of Toledo in front of them, with its rock-colored stone buildings and above them, the light beige fabrics, offering very little protection against the sun and sandstorms.

James lands in front of the main entrance of the city.

Like the first time, they are welcomed by the same Red Army battalion, composed of a good hundred men and women with their weapons conspicuously present.

As they leave, they see the Commander in the front row, waiting for them.

The Eight haven't been gone for a long time; it was just a few days, but it seems to have been an eternity. Even the Commander looks different. Chris can see an orange color above him, a sign of strong agitation. This time, as they all obviously want to go to the party and spend the night there, the Eight move forward to meet him.

"So, what's new since last time, Commander?" asks Jesse in a playful tone.

"Just a lot of pressure from your father all week."

"Did he miss us that much?"

"It would indeed seem so," he replies smiling.

Chris sees the orange color disappearing and returning to a calmer blue. "He will be able to reassure them," he thinks. And then, driven by a very strong intuition, he asks, "Commander is there any way to hide our shuttle somewhere? It's not small, I know, but think it's a precaution worth taking."

The Commander thinks for a few seconds before answering.

"There's an old warehouse a little further away which looks abandoned. We hide strategic products there, if necessary. I can ask someone to come with you if the shuttle can get there."

"That will be perfect. James, are you coming to help me?"

"Why don't we all go and get a few things?" James replies.

"Okay," Jesse says. "Commander, we're going to stay in the city tonight. We'd like to see the Rebels' area again. We want to check out a few things. You can tell my father that we'll all leave early tomorrow morning to arrive in Kantas City on time."

The Commander gives orders for vehicles to escort them to the warehouse. It is a kilometer away and seems so dilapidated that no one could imagine that the most sophisticated flying vehicle in the Red World is hiding inside.

"You want to scare the hell out of us or what, Chris?" asks Stephanie.

"I don't know, it just came to me like that. I am very excited about tonight, but..."

"But what? What?"

"If we could take some weapons with us, I'd feel better."

"Okay. Now I'm scared to death."

"And I'm super excited," Jesse adds.

"And you, you're so sick," Leah says to him.

"Heal me, my dear, heal me," he says, pretending to faint.

Everyone starts laughing while taking large backpacks full of weapons.

"Anyway, we can always give them away," adds Cathy. "Because we'll be going back to Kantas City tomorrow."

"Back to Kantas City," exclaims Max. "But we just left, didn't we?"

"Finally, we'll be back. It seems like an eternity to me," Tabitha replies.

"That's because you don't appreciate freedom, Princess."

She sticks out her tongue, with a teasing look. Max laughs at seeing her like that.

"I think you're off to have a good time tonight."

This time, she kicks him.

"Come on, kids," Cathy laughs. "Let's go!"

They disembark and run to the entrance. They breathe in the smell of sand and its usual warmth.

They are at home here in the Red World.

This time they run to the main square, without any precautions. What they find there exceeds their expectations. The market and its stalls have been replaced by boards serving as tables. This is where the city's inhabitants gather, from the youngest to the oldest. In the middle of the square, musical instruments are set up. Nothing sophisticated, they notice, but enough to make a lot of noise. A kind of marching band welcomes them with a strong lively rhythm that makes everyone smile. Many applaud them. Some come forward to shake their hands. What a contrast to their arrival the first time, only a week ago!

Finally, Poseidon approaches them and takes them in his arms, embracing Tabitha a little longer than the others. Cathy, who is right behind her, immediately notices this and can't help but kick her playfully. Tabitha turns around and winks at her, to Cathy's great satisfaction, happy to see her friend relax.

Poseidon gives a sign for the music to stop. He raises his glass and gives a toast to the Eight and their return. At this signal, the music resumes. The marching band is replaced by much more sophisticated sounds. Max immediately raises his arms to the sky, takes hold of Stephanie and Leah, and leads them into a wild dance. They are joined by Chris, Jesse, and most of the men and women around them.

Poseidon never stops looking at Tabitha.

It is she who then approaches him. She takes his hand. Poseidon's gaze remains attached to her hazel eyes. Hypnotized by each other, they begin to dance.

Cathy and James stand there, watching this unlikely couple form in front of them. Cathy starts laughing, and says to James:

"Come on, my friend. Tonight, we're going to have a party!"

And they both join Max and the others.

They've been dancing for hours. Many children have either returned to their barracks or are sleeping on the ground. The young people are all drunk. The Elites just keep laughing and having fun.

They enjoy their freedom, madness, simplicity combined with decadence, warmth, and aromas.

Then, Chris freezes.

He squats down and puts his hands on his temples. Unbearable pain strikes him; anguish rises within him until he can no longer breathe. Then comes the worst, the vision.

"Poseidon!" he shouts. "Evacuate the area. Take all the children away. Quickly! Quickly!"

The Elites immediately rush to all the vulnerable people—pregnant women, children, the elderly—and lead them to the houses. Poseidon gives orders to those who are still able to fight. James lifts the sleeping children over his shoulders.

Then come the bombs.

The carnage, the screams, the tears.

Their weapons are useless against the military power that strikes them.

The bombs fall one after the other and smoke spreads with each explosion, blocking all visibility. They strike the square, the houses, all over the city. The light beige blanket that once covered the city no longer exists and bits of fabric are flying everywhere.

It's like artificial snow, a little piece of poetry in the middle of the carnage.

James, zigzagging between the explosions, finally finds his backpack in the middle of the square. He pulls out a mini-missile launcher. With a precise and quick shot, he manages to hit a helicopter that was coming towards them. A few seconds later, an explosion is heard. James is getting ready to shoot again, helped by Jesse and Cathy. But the first shot must have had the desired effect because the bombing stops immediately.

Only the carnage, the screams, and the tears remain.

Then come the odors.

Burning. Blood. Fear.

"Chris!" screams Stephanie. "Chris! Chris!"

Chris is lying in the middle of the square. Stephanie is kneeling over him, her hands clasping his beloved face.

"I'm coming, Chris," shouts Leah.

"Chris, Chris, Chris," sobs Stephanie.

"I'm here," says Leah, finally reaching her friends.

"Your hands are shaking," Stephanie whimpers. "You need to focus."

Stephanie turns to Chris again.

"I love you, Chris. You can't leave us now."

The other Elites, Poseidon and some of his relatives, join them in the center of the square. On all their faces, joy has been replaced by anguish. They look at Leah moving her hands over Chris, and Stephanie holding her friend's head.

"Tell him you love him," Leah says to Stephanie.

Stephanie moves closer to Chris' ear and whispers the words to him.

Chris raises his head all of a sudden.

"Is that it, are they gone?" he asks.

Stephanie hugs him, followed by Leah.

"What's going on, girls?" asks Chris.

"Are you all right, old man?" says Max.

"It's a good thing you woke up," Jesse says to Chris. "A little longer and we would have had to stay here forever, because of you!"

"Exactly," James adds, with a big smile. "You scared the hell out of us!"

The anguish they have all felt in the last few minutes is replaced by relief.

"In fact, a big Thank You, James," says Poseidon. "If you hadn't had that missile launcher with you, we might not all be here."

"We can all thank Chris. He's the one who told me to put that gun in my bag. Your power, Chris, is getting stronger and stronger."

"It's a burden. It was terrible what I saw," replies Chris.

"These bombs were not dropped here by chance," says Cathy. "Those who did it knew exactly where we were. They also knew how to cause as much damage and death as possible. Without Chris' intervention, it is not certain that we would all still be here."

"We have to go and see the debris from the helicopter I hit," says James. "Chris, Stephanie, will you come with me?"

"I am taking Tabitha," Jesse says, "We're going to see the Commander."

"I'll go with you too," Cathy suggests. "In case it's another trap."

"Max and I will take care of the injured," says Leah.

"They hit all over the city", Poseidon says. "I'm going to go check on my mother, Beatrix. She stayed in her house in bed. I hope she was able to protect herself. We'll all meet back here in exactly fifteen minutes."

They're about to split up when Poseidon puts a hand on Tabitha's arm. He draws her towards him, first puts his forehead against hers, and then gently kisses her. Time seems to stand still, as if this kiss, long and sweet, were their last.

Finally, he releases her and leaves, without turning back, towards Beatrix's house.

Fifteen minutes have passed.

Leah and Max have rescued, healed, and given endless comfort to the wounded and dying around them. Their uniforms are covered in blood and they appear to have aged a few years in just a few minutes. There are so many wounded.

Tabitha, Cathy, and Jesse return, followed by James, Chris, and Stephanie.

"Who were our assailants?" Cathy asks hastily.

"I have no idea," James replies. "There's no trace of the helicopter left."

"And you? Any clues from the Commander?"

"Unbelievable!" replies Jesse. "They also pounded the Army quarters. The Commander swears that the helicopters were not from our place and that they had never seen them before."

"But we still have doubts," Cathy adds.

"And you?" James asks Leah and Max.

Leah and Max don't answer right away.

Finally, it's Max who talks.

"We have seen children shredded, pregnant women gutted, mothers crying, old people walking around in a state of madness."

The friends look at each other without saying a word, too shocked to add anything.

Abruptly, Poseidon arrives. In his eyes, something has changed.

Tabitha rushes towards him and takes him in her arms.

"Beatrix is dead," he says between sobs.

James and Leah each take one of Cathy's hands without a word.

They remain motionless for a few minutes. Then, like robots, they leave, following Max and Leah, to help heal, comfort and start cleaning up the city.

Toledo, so joyful a few hours ago, is now nothing more than a land of sorrow.

Day 10 of the trip, year 2125

The sun has begun to shine on the square, signaling the Elites that they have to return to their shuttle.

They leave the city to find the sand of the desert in front of them and the old hangar. The Commander is no longer here to wait for them. He now has other concerns to deal with.

The shuttle is intact.

Coming back in this familiar shuttle is a shock, as the last few hours have been really hard on them. They decide they will still leave, to reach Kantas City as soon as possible.

They take advantage of the trip and these last few minutes to remember the beautiful and extraordinary encounters they had during these ten days—experiences that have changed them forever.

They think of Zeus, Noah, Leo and Cathy's mother.

Poseidon, Beatrix, and their Rebel companions.

The elderly lady on the island and her granddaughter, as well as the white man and his Mark.

Michelle, Tiff, Zayn, Tom, and the others in the Valley.

Ellen and her friends on the islands.

They also think of the little diabetic girl who died, and of her mother, and of their people, hidden somewhere in the mountains.

"There are several worlds that are compartmentalized," says Stephanie. "We now know, at least, that in the Red World and the Yellow World, those who do not live in cities must be exterminated. Those in the Valley appear to be protected but cannot go more than one kilometer without also being slaughtered."

"The utopia of our Red World has clearly derailed in recent years," says Max.

"We're going to have to discover these other worlds," adds Leah.

"Above all, we have to find out who shot at us," says James with rage.

"And who is in cahoots with whom, in the Government and in the Red World," adds Cathy.

"We are not the only ones carrying the Mark," says Chris.

"Who are we anyway?" asks Leah.

Leah takes out the statuette she received in Canfranc.

"I kept you close to me because I was hoping you would protect us. You did it, but you didn't tell us all your secrets!"

The Dome is now taking shape in front of them—a modern cupola in the middle of the desert. Through it, they can distinguish the perfectly ordered buildings, and further on, the chaos of the Obama district—a dark spot in this architectural splendor.

"I think we all know what we're going to do when we get back to Kantas City, don't we?" asks Jesse.

"Absolutely," replies Cathy. "We will take over the power and control the Red World."

To be continued in Volume 2

AKNOWLEDGMENTS

I'VE ALWAYS DREAMED OF writing a book.

Partly, because books have accompanied me at every stage of my life, particularly during difficult times. But also, quite simply because I wanted to contribute to this incredible world of imagination.

My wonderful husband gave me the opportunity to embark on this journey, through his unfailing support and thanks to the strength of our partnership that allows us to turn each of our dreams into reality.

Our children, Adelaide and Sebastian, are my main source of inspiration. Adelaide was the only one to read each chapter as they evolved and, starting at just ten years old, she was my first reviewer and kept challenging me with unique ideas. Sebastian is the sun that inspires me to fly higher than ever before.

For this project, I surrounded myself with people I love – they are my family and some of my best friends – because together it's better.

I formed a group of strong and intelligent women who did an extraordinary job of proofreading: Natacha, Aline, Mathilde, Mélanie C-R., Régine, Lucie, Hélène and Mélanie M-U. There is a part of each of you in this book and I can never thank you enough for being next to me in this adventure.

I wrote this book in French, but I wanted to publish it in English. I wouldn't have succeeded in this feat without the help of Gina and Tiffany.

This book is for all those fighting to save our beautiful planet.

* D I D 2 5 4 7 2 5 6 *
L - #0092 - 210619 - C0 - 210/148/13 - PB - DID2547256